Hapenny Magick

Hapenny Magick

Jennifer Carson

SPENCER HILL
MIDDLE GRADE

Spencer Hill Press

Contact: Spencer Hill Press, PO Box 247, Contoocook, NH 03229,
USA

Please visit our website at www.spencerhillpress.com

First Edition: December 2011
Second Edition: April 2014

Carson, Jennifer, 1975

Hapenny Magick : a novel / by Jennifer Carson - 2nd ed.
p. cm.
Summary: The smallest hapenny must find a way
to save her village from a troll invasion.

Cover design and interior illustrations
by Patricia Ann Lewis-MacDougall

ISBN 978-1-937053-91-8 (Paperback)
ISBN 978-1-937053-86-4 (e-book)

Printed in the United States of America

For all those who believe in finding the magick in every day.

For Mrs. McNaughton
and her fabulous readers!

Shine Brightly!

Jennifer Carson

Chapter One

Mae peered out the front door, scanning the forest at the edge of the farm. Mother Underknoll had been missing for a week, and rumors of troll sightings near the village were spreading like poison ivy. She scratched at an itchy spot and pulled a tick from the fur on the back of her ear.

The mud squished between her toes as Mae headed for the henhouse. Mist clung to the still morning air, making her hair curl like a goat's beard. The rising sun dappled the bark of the tree her home was built beneath.

She rolled up her frayed sleeves, the cuffs soft and worn from many washings. Mae unlatched the henhouse door and pushed it open on creaky hinges. She pulled the stool along, its legs squeaking across the wooden floor. The basket for gathering the eggs teetered on the seat as Mae climbed the rungs.

"What have you got for me today, Bernice?" she asked the youngest hen in the brood. The hen had roosted on some peculiar things lately, like rocks and acorns and a red marble Mae thought she'd lost.

Her hand slid under the warm feathers and closed around a single egg.

The hen clucked softly.

"It's okay, Bernice." Mae pulled the egg out from under the hen. "At least it's an egg this time. Soon you'll be laying more eggs than you—"

She stared at the egg in her hand. It was a vibrant shade of purple.

If her guardian, Gelbane, saw it, she'd fly into an all-out, henpecking fit.

Mae's ears perked at the sound of hooves pounding outside the henhouse and her guardian's shrill scream.

"You little twit!" Gelbane screeched from the house. "This is the third time the pigs have escaped this week!"

"Day-old biscuits!" Mae cursed and dropped the purple egg into the basket, jumped off the stool, and scuttled out the door.

The pigpen gate swung on its rusted hinges. The once securely- tied rope dangled from the top crossbar. Piglets chased each other around the well. The boar rooted in the vegetable patch. The sows feasted in the flowerbeds.

Dropping the basket, Mae dove for a squealing piglet. She hugged him so tight his bristly fur pricked through the thin cloth of her dress. The piglet kicked and squirmed as she stumbled under his weight. Mud streaked her clean apron. She tossed the squealer into the pen and slammed the gate shut.

How had the rope come undone? She'd tied it properly this time. She'd even triple knotted it!

Forgetting the escaped piglets, Mae froze as her guardian stormed across the yard.

Gelbane's double chin wobbled. Her tattered, homespun skirt flared. The brass buttons on her green vest flashed. Catching the end of the rope between her sausage-like fingers, Gelbane narrowed her small, dark eyes. "How many times have I shown you how to tie the gate proper-like?"

Mae peered through her thick bangs as she hung her head. "More times than a cow chews its cud, ma'am."

Gelbane looked so cross, Mae thought she saw fangs sprouting out from under her upper lip. She snuck a second peek, just to be sure she'd imagined it.

"Then why do we have piglets trampling the yard again?"

Mae shuffled her feet, toes digging in the soft dirt. She wished she could sink down into the mud and disappear. She sniffled and ran a ragged sleeve under her nose.

"Speak up!" Gelbane screeched.

"I'm sorry, ma'am. I don't know what happened. I tied the gate shut before slopping the pigs like you taught me—"

Gelbane's jaw jutted forward. "If you had done as I taught you, we'd be eating breakfast by now."

Breakfast! Mae scanned the ground. The basket lay tipped on its side, trampled and muddy from the runaway pigs, but the purple egg lay undisturbed in the grass.

Mae hoped her guardian didn't follow her gaze.

"Out of the kindness of my heart, I took you in when your ma took off," Gelbane sneered over her bulbous nose. "I've treated you like my own kin for six long years because your mother was so sweet in my time of need. But you've caused me nothing but grief!"

Tears formed in Mae's eyes, but she blinked them away. She wouldn't let them fall. Her fingers closed around the blue pendant tucked away under her blouse.

Gelbane wiped her hands on her skirt as if even the thought of Mae was disgusting. "You all but stopped growing when your ma took off. It's not like you don't get enough food. Odd you are. Too small and twitchy, even for a hapenny."

Tangled red hair spilled forward as Gelbane bent to poke a finger into Mae's shoulder, punctuating her words. "You'll have no breakfast and no mid-morning bite. I don't care if you starve until midnight nibble. Nothing until you catch all those pigs!"

Mae nodded. "Yes, ma'am."

Gelbane shuffled her vast weight past the pigpen and across the yard; her wide feet made sucking noises as she slogged through the mud and back into the house. Mae gave one last squeeze to the pendant under her blouse and picked up the lone purple egg.

If she threw it at Gelbane's head, what a satisfying splat it would make! But it wasn't worth the beating she'd get afterward. She stomped over to the crumpled basket and settled the egg into the bottom. Her fists clenched into tight balls. She was always getting into trouble for things that weren't her fault.

"So much for starting the day out clean." Mae sighed and flicked the clumps of mud from her apron. She tried to scowl at the pigs, but it just wasn't in her heart to be mad at them. It wasn't their fault she couldn't tie a knot properly.

The farmyard was in shambles. The grass was trampled deep into the mud. The mud had a thousand little ditches from the pigs' hooves. At least the piglets had stopped chasing each other when Gelbane started yelling. Most of them now rooted in the vegetable garden at the edge of the small farm.

"Here, pig-pigs!" Mae called.

She took her mother's old flute from her pocket and turned it in her hand. The sun shone on its walnut finish. It was one of two things belonging to her momma that she'd managed to keep from Gelbane. She was only six when Momma left, but she had been smart enough to know that Gelbane wasn't like the other hapenny villagers.

The pendant was the second thing Mae had managed to keep. It carried a secret inside—a lock of her father's hair. Mae barely remembered him. He was one of many lost on one of the Great Expeditions, two years before her momma went away. No one but Momma had left the safety of the village since, until last week, when Mother Underknoll disappeared.

Chapter Two

Life would be so different if Mae's momma would just come back. Her home would be tidy, the floor swept, the spider webs kept to the too-high corners. Furniture would shine with polish, and the hearth would never go cold. The lacy curtains on the windows wouldn't be tatty or covered in faerie dust. And Mae wouldn't have to hide things away to keep them safe.

The chimney of her home poked out between two large tree roots, but there was no smoke curling from the flue. The fire had gone to ashes during the night. No sparkle was left on the grime-covered window panes, either. Climbing vines grew over the small, round windows, which made it impossible to see if Gelbane was spying on her. On the other hand, Gelbane probably couldn't see Mae, either. She swiveled her ears toward the house and heard banging and cursing. Her guardian was fooling around with another one of her contraptions.

Ever since Mae could remember, Gelbane had tinkered with the making of odd machines. Her latest contraption was made of iron gears that ground with a moan and jaws that snapped with a clang. Gelbane said the machine was to make the grinding of grain into flour faster, but it looked rather more like a torture device than a gristmill, and it had yet to prove itself faster than Mae with a pestle and mortar. In fact, the machine had yet to prove itself at grinding even a single kernel of grain.

Mae flipped her flute over in her hand, losing herself in the gentle curving lines that ran through it. Using her flute was the easiest way to catch the pigs, but if Gelbane caught her, she would surely have to sleep in the barn tonight instead of in her cozy dreaming nook.

She really didn't want to chase down every pig. Not today. Not for the third day in a row. She sighed and put the flute to her lips, blowing a catchy tune. It had enough spirit to get the pigs' attention away from the flowers, but hopefully would not rouse Gelbane's ire.

Gelbane didn't understand how the music could lure the pigs into the pen, and she didn't like Mae doing it. Mae didn't know how it worked, either, but if she was going to catch all the pigs and make Gelbane's breakfast on time, she'd better catch them quickly. And that meant using her flute to do it.

Mae pretended that her flute playing was her own little bit of magick. Her best friend, Leif, said that hapennies had no magick. He said only the wizened Protector of the Wedge, who patrolled the borders of their village and kept the forest trolls away, had magick. Mae was glad the Wedge had a protector to defend it, but she wished hapennies were capable of protecting themselves. She wished she could be a Protector of the Wedge.

Skipping to the tune she played, Mae made her way to the edge of the hayfield. One by one the piglets came, trotting in a line like a gaggle of newly hatched goslings. A sow at the rear kept the piglets in line. The boar took the lead. Mae's skirt swayed against her knees as she led the swine parade. They trotted up the hill that the barn was built into, through the damp and dewy grass, and to the pigpen. Kicking the gate open, Mae danced into the sty.

Most of the pigs were safe once more—except for a few wily piglets and the sow still nipping the heads off the flowers. The sow's head nodded to the beat; she even let out a happy oink, but she didn't join the march through the farmyard. The piglets were always hard to catch, but sometimes one of the sows would go missing for weeks and then show up one morning like she'd never been gone. It was a good thing Gelbane never paid much attention to how many pigs they actually had.

"Looks like those piglets are going to lead you on a merry chase!"

"Oh!" The musical notes floated off into the morning as Mae jerked in surprise. "Leif! You scared me." Her heart did a little tap dance on her ribs. It always did that when Leif was around. She smiled and tucked her hair behind her ear, dropping the flute into the pocket of her apron for safekeeping.

Jumping out of the hayfield, Leif pointed to the piglets. "I can catch them for you, if you want me to."

Leif always tried to be noble, like the hapennies in legend who wore gilded armor and saved ladies in distress. Like the time he'd spent the whole day picking berries for the village baker, Mrs. Birchbeam. It had been the day before Mr. and Mrs. Belowpine's wedding, and Mrs. Birchbeam had been frantic for time, scrambling to and fro to get everything prepared, or so Leif had told Mae. The cake was to be a scrumptious white cake with wedgeberry jelly between the layers and purple frosting flowers decorating the top. Leif had promised to bring her a piece, but he never made it to the wedding. The berry patch he'd foraged in was riddled with poison ivy, and Leif had spent the next week in bed, with cotton mittens on his hands to keep from scarring up his skin when he scratched.

"I can catch them," Mae said. "I don't want to get you in trouble, too."

Bushy brows arched over Leif's sky-blue eyes. He swiped at the ginger curls that bounced over his forehead. "You're already in trouble this morning?"

Mae nodded. She scooped up the trampled basket and put the egg in Leif's hand. "A purple egg! What's wrong with that hen?"

Tossing the egg in the air and catching it again, Leif laughed, a dimple pulling his left cheek. "Strange things happen at your house."

"Well, they've been happening a lot more lately, and it's making Gelbane even crankier than usual." Mae grabbed the egg back from her friend. She wished she could be as unconcerned as Leif. "You know what strange things usually mean." Mae lowered her voice. "A wizard must be in the Wedge."

"Oh, troll dung! There haven't been any wizards actually in the village since the Great Protector, Gythal." He shoved his hands into his pockets and leaned against the barn wall. His eyes sparkled brightly against his copper skin. The fur on his ears shone with golden highlights in the sun. Leif's blue, homespun shirt was new, but he still wore the same patched-up overalls as always. Mae remembered how he got the patch on his left knee, and blushed a little to think about the day he'd saved her from falling into the river.

"What did Gelbane say about the purple egg?" Leif asked.

Mae swallowed. "She didn't notice the egg because the pigs escaped from the pen."

"Again?" Leif slapped his palm against his forehead. "That's the third time this week!"

"That's what she said." Mae scowled. "I don't point out all *your* faults. I just don't understand why the gate keeps coming undone. If I didn't know better, I would think Gelbane does it just for a reason to punish me."

Leif slid his hand into hers. "Hey, Mae, I'm sorry. I'm sure it's not your fault that the pigs got out. There has to be something wrong with the fence."

Mae gave her friend a sad smile. She was pretty sure whatever was wrong with the fence had more to do with her than Leif wanted to believe.

"Come with me and Reed. Momma needs us to go to the market. It's been a really long time since anyone in the village has seen you. Mr. Whiteknoll has been asking where you've been."

Mae thought about the tall village tailor with his spiky white hair and bright eyes. He liked to laugh and sew lace on everything. Her eyes took in the yellow-green grass drooping over the hill and sweeping across the barn doors. She followed the line of fence separating the barnyard from the pigsty and remembered helping her mother dig the holes for the fence posts, and the first piglets they'd brought home from Farmer Burrbridge's. That was the day she'd met Leif. She was four, and he'd told her that he liked the heart-shaped pocket on her apron. They'd been best friends ever since, even though Leif was now fourteen winters and she was only twelve. He'd been the only hapenny to come and visit after her mother left. The others were too afraid of Gelbane.

"Have they found Mother Underknoll yet?"

Leif shook his head. "There's no sign of her. I don't understand why she would leave the Wedge."

"Perhaps she didn't leave—"

"I need my breakfast!" Gelbane's holler bounced off the barn and rang in Mae's ears. Mae cringed as a window slammed shut against a sill.

"How will I ever be able to go with you to the village again?" Mae sighed. "I might as well be chained to the fence post. She never lets me out of her sight anymore." Mae squeezed Leif's hand and then let go.

"We will be fishing at the river later; maybe you can sneak away. Reed just got some new flies." Leif shoved his hands in his pockets and drew pictures in the mud with his toes. His ears flicked at a bee buzzing near. "It's weird the way the fishing flies just appear on our doorstep."

"See?" Mae gave his shoulder a friendly punch. "It's not just my house where strange things happen. Tell Mr. Whiteknoll I'll visit as soon as I can."

Leif bit his lip. "Before I go...I made something for you." He took his hand from his pocket and uncurled his fingers.

Mae picked up the wooden bird from his palm. It was a raven with its wings spreading out from its body, head posed high. She held it up and studied the finely carved lines. The

wood was almost as soft as a pat of warm butter. "He's magnificent! Look at his eyes! It's like he could come alive in my hand."

A dimple puckered Leif's cheek as he grinned. "A bunch of ravens have been gathering in our cornfield lately, so I got to study them real close. I'm glad you like it."

"I love it!" Mae threw her arms around her friend.

Leif dropped his head and quickly kissed her on the cheek. When he pulled back, his cheeks were strawberry red. "See you later, Mae!"

As he trotted around the barn, Mae touched the spot where Leif's lips had left behind a bit of moisture; he'd never kissed her before! She waved as he trotted through the field. She had to get to the bridge this afternoon. Perhaps she could sneak away like Leif suggested. Maybe she could lull Gelbane to sleep with a lullaby. If the flute worked on the pigs, perhaps it would work on her guardian as well.

After stowing the raven in her pocket until she could find a safe hiding place for it, Mae looped the rope around the pigpen gate and tied the knot exactly as Gelbane had taught her, daring it to come undone. She glanced at the flower-eating sow. She should've taken Leif up on his offer to help catch the remaining pigs. The sow winked and grinned as if reading Mae's mind. Mae shook her head; first Gelbane's fangs, now a winking pig—her eyes must be playing tricks on her today.

"My breakfast, NOW!" Gelbane shrieked from the house. "Or you'll get the whip just for my amusement!"

As fast as she could, Mae scampered across the farmyard.

Chapter Three

Stars shone in the deep velvet sky as Mae lay back in the hay. It had been a long day. Window washing, floor scrubbing, stall mucking, sock darning. The work was never-ending. And then Gelbane had made Mae choose between supper and the new letter that had come in the post from her mother. Mae's stomach churned and gurgled. It really wasn't a choice.

A piglet nestled against Mae and snuffled in her ear, its breath warm and damp. She patted his bristly back. "I'm glad to be snuggling with you, too, pig-pig."

Being in the barn was almost better than sleeping in the house with Gelbane, but she yearned for her cozy dreaming nook. And she missed tucking the frayed ends of her old blanket under her chin. At least the pigs didn't snore.

Pulling the newest letter from her pocket, Mae unfolded the stiff paper. The letters were scrawled across the page in a loose calligraphy.

My Dearest One,

I dream of you at night, and your father, who I am still searching for. The search has been in vain, I fear, but I will not give up, as I hope you will not give up on me returning to you. Be good for Gelbane, do as you are bid. You must be getting so grown up now. Until I find the time to write again,

Your Mother

Mae thought of Mabel, Mother Underknoll's newly born, as she let the letter fall from her fingers. Would Mabel grow up wishing for her momma the way Mae did? At least Mabel still had her father and not just a lock of his hair. Mae only had memories of her parents to cling to. She was six when her momma left, too young to understand why Momma was leaving. But after she went away, odd things started happening at Mae's house. Pumpkins growing with jack-o'-lantern faces, knots untying themselves, and now chickens laying purple eggs. Mae couldn't explain any of it. Or why it was happening far too often nowadays.

The piglet gave Mae a sidelong glance when her belly grumbled again. "Sorry. I can skip breakfast, but it's torture to miss noon meal, high tea, supper, and midnight nibble. I spent all day doing chores or trying to catch you piglets."

Mae rubbed her sore backside, trying to forget the paddling she'd received. A few piglets were worth much more to Gelbane than an abandoned hapenny.

The pigs settled into the hay, and Mae gazed out through the window high above. The full moon lit the inside of the barn like a table full of blazing candles. She pulled her flute from her apron pocket and rubbed the smooth finish with her thumb. How she wished she could remember all the songs her mother used to play. But she only remembered one.

Putting her fingers to the flute, Mae filled the barn with a sleepy tune. It was the lullaby every hapenny mother sang to comfort her little ones. The one she was going to try on Gelbane, if she ever got the chance. Mae knew every word and every note. She could almost hear her mother's lilting voice singing in harmony.

> Soft sleep, my little hapenny
> Outside, "Goodnight," the owls call
> I'll tuck you safely in your bed
> Protector of the Wedge watches over all
> His magick watches over all.
>
> The wind will sing a lullaby
> Nod, oh nod, your head
> While stars are slowly drifting by
> Dream sweetly in your bed
> Dream sweetly in your bed.
>
> Soft sleep, my little hapenny
> Outside, "Goodnight," the owls call
> I'll tuck you safely in your bed
> Protector of the Wedge watches over all
> His magick watches over all
> His magick watches over all.

Spotting a spider web clinging to the rafters, Mae dropped the flute on her chest and reached to trace the shining strands with a finger. It was too high to actually touch, but she pretended. Each time she pointed to an anchor strand, it sparkled brightly.

Halfway through the tracing of the spider's complicated design a black bird flapped through the window. It had a long, curving beak and feathers that stuck out haphazardly on its chest. It settled on a wooden beam, cocking its head back and forth, as if trying to get a good look at her.

"Hello," Mae said. Her voice trembled a little. Her ears pressed flat against her head. The black gaze of a raven could be a bit frightening. "Hello, my mighty friend."

The bird shifted his feet on the beam. "Hello, Maewyn."

Mae sat upright. The flute rolled into the hay. Her heart pounded in her ears. She stared open-mouthed. "You can talk?"

Mae had heard tales of birds that could talk, but she'd never met one. Before the Great Troll Invasion, hapennies had welcomed the occasional visit from a traveling minstrel, and she remembered hearing stories of high adventure on the sea, adventures hapennies would never dare. In the stories, the great men kept birds as pets, and taught them to speak, and sent them off to scout for land when supplies were low.

The raven glided to where Mae sat and folded his wings against his body. He looked like the carving Leif had given her this morning. She felt her pocket. The carving was still there. As she reached out with a shaking hand to touch the silky feathers, she wondered if he was one of the birds from the Burrbridge's cornfield. He pressed his head against her palm and then hopped back, gesturing with his wing. "Come, Maewyn."

"Come?" It was strange enough that the bird was talking, but now he wanted her to follow him? Mae narrowed her eyes and pursed her lips. "Come where?"

"Come." The raven flapped back up to the rafters and then to the sill of the open window high above.

Mae had so many questions. How did this raven learn to talk? How did he know her name? How could she ignore him?

There was light from a full moon, and Mae knew the Wedge like she knew the skin of an apple. She would make sure she was back before dawn, before Gelbane had a reason to check on her. The raven took flight, heading for the forest. Mae jumped up, ran to the door, and pushed it open to the chill night air.

She paused to look back at the piglets, all snuggled together. What if she didn't return before the sun rose? Would Gelbane take her anger out on the pigs? Would she use the whip instead of her hand on Mae's backside next time, or shackle Mae as she'd threatened before? Mae swallowed, indecision swirling in her mind. "It couldn't be any worse than today, right, pig-pig?"

The piglet snuffled, rubbing its snout against the warm hay she'd left behind.

"Right. I'll be back in two flicks of a goat's ear!" Mae scampered across the yard and onto the trail that led through the field at the edge of the forest. Few had traveled this road since the disappearance of those in the Great Expedition.

Her feet pattered against the dirt path, and Mae hesitated as she arrived at the far reaches of her village, known as the Wedge. The only bridge leading from the mainland to the hapenny island arched over the rushing river that separated the two. The protective runes on the pillars held shadows in the moonlight. Mae shivered at the sight of the tall stones looming on the riverbank. The stones were trolls that had tried to cross the bridge. The rune magick had turned them into lumpy granite sentinels. The Wedge's Protector must have left the stone trolls there as a warning to other invaders; perhaps it was a warning for adventurous hapennies as well.

"Come, Maewyn!" the raven called.

Mae shifted from foot to foot with indecision. She was safe in the Wedge—safe from trolls. Those hairy, drooling beasts liked to eat hapennies. Her nose twitched with nervousness. Her ears swiveled, listening for strange sounds in the night. The closest she'd ever come to crossing the bridge was fishing beside it with Leif and Reed. On the other hand, a bird had never talked to her before. Mae dashed across the planks before she could change her mind.

Bright eyes peered at her over swells in the land. She hoped the eyes belonged to owls or opossums and not to something more frightening. She scurried over fallen trees, hands brushing across soft moss. A shiver ran through her, and she wrapped her arms around herself. She'd never been alone in the forest at night. Every once in a while, the trees would thin, and she could see the moon shining at the top of the world, like the round, weighted end of a clock pendulum. Mae picked up her pace and sprinted across a meadow glittering with dew.

When the hem of her skirt was sodden and heavy, Mae stopped, plopped onto a tree stump, and rubbed her chilled, wet toes. She'd come so far from the Wedge. Would she be able to find her way back?

The raven alighted on a nearby boulder.

"We've traveled so far already," Mae said. "What is it you want me to see?"

The bird flew off once again, calling for her to follow.

Mae slouched and crossed her arms over her chest. "Why should I?"

A cool breeze wound through the trees and a twig cracked somewhere nearby. Mae jumped from her perch, forgetting about her chilled toes, and sprinted after the raven. She didn't dare look back.

The air was heavy with the fragrance of wet leaves and pine needles. Mae stumbled over tree roots, and her apron snagged on the thorns of budding raspberry bushes. The stars had traveled halfway across the sky when Mae found herself near a babbling creek.

She knelt to drink from the dark water, not even bothering to cup her hand, but slurping straight from the current. She had followed the raven too far. She should turn around now, even though there was no hope of being home before Gelbane discovered her missing. Mae strengthened her resolve to face the fact that she would get more than just a few chilly nights in the barn and a hungry belly. She would lose hide from her backside, of that she was sure. And for what? A midnight stroll in the forest with a bossy bird.

Lifting her head to wipe the dribbles of water from her face, Mae saw a path made of stones, going through the creek. The wet faces of the rocks glistened. She followed the path with her eyes.

Chapter Four

Just beyond the creek, a cozy cabin nestled within a grove of oaks. It wasn't the dwelling of a hapenny, of that Mae was sure. Hapennies always built their homes under something: hills, bridges, stones, or ancient trees. A thin tendril of smoke, like dragon's breath, curled over the thatched roof.

The raven settled on the cabin's stone chimney. Uneven granite stairs led to a small covered porch. Under the single front window, a long planting box overflowed with night-blooming flowers. The pale petals basked in the glow of the yellow moon. The door to the cottage was open, and Mae saw a man at the hearth.

She crossed the creek and crept closer.

The man in the cottage was tall, with a long, ginger beard. His garments were not rich, but they were clean and serviceable. His breeches were the color of plums, his linen shirt a spinach green. Shiny buttons connected his suspenders to his waistband.

"Maewyn, come," the raven called.

The bird glided from the chimney, went through the open door, and landed on the rounded back of an overstuffed chair. Ducking behind a tree for cover, Mae wondered why the raven had led her here. A woodsman's cottage!

The man approached the raven, his leather-clad feet shushing across the wood plank floor. "Where have you been, my friend?"

Mae saw affection in his face as the woodsman scratched under the raven's beak. To treat a bird like that, he had to be better than Gelbane. Perhaps he wasn't a woodsman after all. Maybe he was the Wedge's Protector. A wizard would have a talking bird as sure as a hapenny would have a lavender honey muffin recipe. Perhaps he could explain the odd things happening at the farm. Mae stepped out from behind the tree.

The raven cocked his head. The man followed the bird's gaze. "Maewyn," the bird called. It felt like an introduction.

Hesitantly, Mae gathered her skirts, her foot lifting to find the first stair. Soft light from the fire fell on her face. The mouth-watering smell of fowl and roasting vegetables teased her nose. The juices from the roast sizzled on the hot coals. Something bubbled in a pot over the fire. Mae hadn't eaten since supper the day before. Her stomach called out for nourishment.

Mae lifted her eyes to the man. The end of his beard was braided like a pack pony's tail, with a thin red ribbon holding it together. The nose that protruded over the beard was broad and squashed at the tip. What should she say? She wound the corner of her apron around her thumb.

"Please, sir, I have walked all night." Mae pointed to the raven perched on the chair and her belly grumbled again. "That bird led me here."

The man chuckled, and Mae felt embarrassment crawl up her neck like a tomato vine growing up a fence post. She was foolish to think a human would ever believe that a bird led her through the forest. Foolish to think a human would be better than the worst-tempered hapenny. Foolish to think this man could possibly be the Protector of the Wedge.

Hugging herself, Mae turned from the door and the fire. She would find her way back through the forest. Back to the dishes and the scrubbing of floors. Back to the feeding of chickens. Back to Gelbane.

"Maewyn."

Mae started at the man's deep voice.

"Come back." Laughter filled the space between them. "Come back, Maewyn. I wasn't laughing at you. I forgot hapennies always take things so close to heart. I was just... wasn't expecting a...hap—well, just wasn't expecting you. That's all." He held out his hand. "It is nice to meet you, Maewyn."

Mae reached for the long fingers. The man's grasp was warm as it closed around her hand.

Skin the color of brewed tea crinkled around hazel eyes. Freckles tiptoed across the wide bridge of his nose. In the brim of the man's hat, a small furry creature was curled, asleep. "Are you the Protector of the Wedge?"

"Some call me that."

"What do the others call you?"

The man chuckled softly. "Callum. The others call me Callum, and so can you." He let her hand fall from his. "I have a lovely partridge roast and some vegetable soup, but it needs a few more minutes to simmer. Would you like some fresh bread?"

Mae nodded. She had always just accepted what was given; never had Gelbane asked what she would like.

Callum gestured for Mae to follow as he loped down the steps with an easy gait. She had to run to keep up with his long stride. Callum pointed to a meadow behind the cottage. "Do you see the wheat stalks?"

Mae nodded. They looked like pale shafts of moonlight rising from the earth. But this wasn't the right time for wheat!

Callum gathered ripe kernels from the stalks, took Mae's hand, and turned it over in his grasp. He placed the kernels in her open palm. She ran her thumb over their rough surface while Callum strolled to the creek. To make bread you had to have flour, and flour came from grinding wheat kernels into powder. She'd learned that much from Mrs. Birchbeam, the village baker. But how were they going to make bread in time for supper? It needed time to rise.

Returning with a handful of water, Callum dribbled it on the grains. Mae swallowed hard as the kernels grew warm in her hand. Her heart pittered against her ribs. She wasn't sure what to expect.

Using the braided end of his beard like a wand, Callum swirled it above the wheat kernels. "A sweetened loaf is the prize. Grains of flour, quickly rise!"

The kernels wiggled and danced. Water swirled and steamed. Mae's nose twitched with the smell of fresh bread. She watched in awe as the kernels expanded, the hard hulls falling away. Soon Mae held a small, browned loaf of bread. Her mouth watered as a pat of butter appeared and melted over the crusty surface.

"Go on, eat it," Callum said with a wave of his hand. He turned and strolled back to the fire-lit cottage.

Mae pulled off the end of the loaf and stuffed it into her mouth. The bite was warm and soft, and it didn't hurt her teeth like the stale barley bread she'd always had to eat. "Thank you, sir," she mumbled through a mouthful.

"It was the least I could do after you've come so far," Callum said. "Are you coming in or not?"

Mae skipped back up to the cottage. By the time she reached the first step, the loaf was nearly gone. When she reached the threshold, she swallowed the last bite. As she entered the cottage, her curiosity grew bigger than her hunger.

Chapter Five

Books were stacked everywhere, with titles on the spines like *Badabing's Cache of Spells, Pognut's Potions and Brews, and Ahem's Book of Proper Grammar for Spell Casting.*

Mae's mother had owned a lot of books, too. Gelbane had used most for kindling, but Mae was able to sneak a few away and hide them in the rafters of the barn. She'd read those few stories over and over again, until she could nearly recite them by heart. The only book Gelbane had kept was The Hapenny Farmer's Guide to Pig Wifery and Husbanding. It was a large tome explaining the finer points of swine breeding. Gelbane had recited the first rule: "Never breed a pig during a full moon." Leif's dad, Farmer Burrbridge, said that full-moon piglets would turn feral and grow tusks. Mae wasn't sure if he was teasing her when he told her that, but Mae never touched the book without Gelbane's permission, and then only to wipe the soot from its cover, so she hadn't had a chance to read the truth.

A red, oversized chair stuffed full to bursting sat close to the hearth, with an oval-shaped rug on the floor in front of it made from loops of colorful fabric. Mae was pretty sure she saw a fancy-dressed critter scurry under a tall cabinet in the corner. She dropped to her knees and peeked under, but only caught sight of little footprints in the dust. "What was that?"

Callum ladled soup into a small bowl. "You mean, 'Who was that?' That was Trina. She'll come out and introduce herself when she's ready. She's a bit shy, like all red squirrels." Callum pointed to the furry critter in his hat brim. "This is Beau, her brother. He's a bit braver and already sneaking curious peeks at you, I'm sure."

Over the brim of the wizard's hat Mae spotted two gleaming eyes, peering at her as she brushed the dust from her skirt. She moved toward the crackling fire and sat on the hearth, and Callum handed her a bowl of soup along with a wooden spoon. The spoon was carved from a twisted twig and worn smooth from use. It was much fancier than the spoons she used at her house. Mae dipped into the broth and sipped.

The sweet taste of onions and potatoes was bliss. She grinned as Callum slipped a piece of partridge into her bowl. Her supper usually consisted of watery cabbage, with bits of tough old chicken thrown in when one of the hens refused to lay more eggs. Mae gobbled the meal down like a pig at a trough.

Callum sat in the overstuffed chair watching Mae. She ate the last spoonful and wished she had a piece of bread left over to sop up the last licks of broth. She sighed with contentment, full for the first time in months. The wizard took the empty bowl and set it on the narrow table near his chair. "How was your supper?"

Mae smiled. "It was the best meal ever!"

"Food is kind of my specialty," Callum said.

"Thank you, sir." Mae leaned against the hearth. The stones were warm from the fire and soothing against her tired body. Her eyelids were heavy. It would be so nice to fall asleep, but Mae knew she would have to go home soon. She wasn't looking forward to another wet trek through the woods.

The raven flew to Callum and settled on his shoulder. The wizard patted the bird without much thought. Then, leaning forward in his chair, Callum swung his arms forward to rest on his knees. "I take it your life with Gelbane has been a little, uh, unpleasant."

Mae's gaze flicked from the man's stare to the raven perched on his shoulder. She shook her head, dropping her gaze to the floor. She followed the curving paths of the wood grain with a finger. "How do you know about Gelbane?"

Callum lifted the front brim of his hat off his head and scratched his scalp. "She's been your guardian since your mother left, hasn't she?"

"Yes."

"She treats you like her servant."

"I don't want to be a bother to anyone, sir." Mae twisted the corners of her apron. "She was kind enough to take me in."

"Hogwash! We both know that Gelbane is anything but kind."

Tears gathered on Mae's lashes. She didn't like to wallow in her sorrows. What was the wizard trying to get at, anyway?

Callum's voice softened. "Your mother was very kind to invite Gelbane to share your home after her village was invaded by trolls. It's too bad your mother isn't around to see what a fine young lady you've become, despite Gelbane's dreadful treatment."

The tears that had gathered now hurried down Mae's cheeks. She didn't swipe them away. "I miss her. I wish she would come home." The raven hopped from Callum's shoulder to the top of the chair and settled to preen his ebony feathers. Mae brushed at the dried mud on her toes. Her ears hung low. "Sometimes, I think it was my fault that she left."

Shaking his head, Callum clicked his tongue. "Her leaving had nothing to do with you." He lifted Mae's chin with a finger, his hazel gaze intense. "I know about the wonderful things that happen around you, Maewyn."

Mae narrowed her eyes. "What do you mean?"

"Hens laying purple eggs, flowers blooming in the winter—"

"Waking up with my hair in knots, gates coming unlatched," Mae scoffed, and pulled her chin from the wizard's grasp. "I don't think those things are so wonderful. I need you to tell me how to stop them. That's why the raven led me here, isn't it?"

"Magick can be wonderful, Maewyn, if you know how to use it. The raven brought you here, not to stop these things, but to help you learn how to control them. Perhaps you are even to be the next Protector of the Wedge."

"That's ridiculous. A wizard must protect the Wedge, not a hapenny." Mae yawned and stretched her legs. "We are too small...especially me."

"Magick is not limited by size or species. Why, the Great Protector, Gythal, was just a tiny man himself, and he's the one responsible for putting the protective runes on the bridge to keep the trolls out of the Wedge. Right, old boy?"

The raven shook his body and flapped his wings, letting out a loud croak.

Callum cleared his throat. His voice grew serious again. "For you to be born with such magick, there must be a reason."

"There's never been a hapenny with magick before. Why would there be one now? Why would it be me? I'm the smallest hapenny in the Wedge!"

"Wizards show up where they are needed," Callum said. "And that's about all the explanation I can give you. We don't choose to have magick. It chooses us."

"But we have a Protector," Mae insisted. "We have you." Leif always said that hapennies didn't have magick. Could he be wrong? Were the strange things that happened on the farm really her uncontrolled magick?

"Yes, well, I won't live forever. Wizard or not, I'm still a mortal man." Callum shifted in his chair and peered at the half-open door. "Did you hear that?"

Mae's ears swiveled forward. Her nose twitched with fright. Gelbane must have noticed she was missing. Perhaps she had tracked her through the woods. What would happen if her guardian found her here? Mae's muscles tightened, ready to flee.

Footsteps clicked on the stairs. The door creaked open. A pink nose appeared, followed by two dark eyes. Mae's shoulders slumped with relief as the flower-eating sow trotted into the cottage. "Oh, pig-pig, it's you!" She ran to the pig and patted her head. "I got into lots of trouble because of you—"

Callum closed the door behind the sow. "Aletta, there you are. It took you long enough."

Mae looked at Callum. "Aletta? You know this pig?"

The sow snorted and stood on her hind legs. Mae leaped back as dark hair sprouted from the top of the pig's head. Hooves turned into stubby fingers and toes. Pink skin turned into a light pink chemise with a mauve overdress. The wizard stretched her arms and yawned as her snout shrank into a pert nose. "That is the last time I spend two weeks as a pig. Snort,

snort!" Aletta covered her mouth with her hands as her cheeks blushed bright red. "Oh, excuse me! Side effect, you know!"

Mae stared in astonishment. The woman was stout, but moved across the room with grace, grabbing a bowl from the table as she passed. She scooped a ladleful of stew into the bowl and brought it to her nose.

Callum gently closed Mae's mouth with a finger under her chin.

"Ah, wonderful stuff. I've looked forward to eating something besides slop and flowers for days." Aletta slurped the stew, not even bothering with a spoon.

Mae tugged at Callum's sleeve, pointing at Aletta. "Can all wizards do that?"

Callum shook his head. "You should always use utensils."

"No," Mae giggled, "will I be able to change myself into a pig?"

Aletta put her hand on her hip. Callum wrinkled his nose. As if reading each other's minds, they asked in unison, "Why would you want to?"

Mae pointed at the raven perched on the chair. "Any animal, really. If I am a wizard, will I be able to...transform into an animal?"

"Verdan Gripora?" Callum shrugged. "That's advanced magick, but perhaps, if Aletta feels you have the talent."

"Is the raven a wizard, too?" Mae looked up at Callum. "Why hasn't he changed yet?"

Callum smiled, but his eyes were sad. "He's a bit like a Protector, but he's not going to change from being a raven. We call him Remy."

"Not all wizards have talent in all areas," Aletta said, taking Mae by the shoulders and leading her back to the fire. "Some, like me, are gifted at changing form; some are talented with

plants. Others are good with animals or music or potions. We all have our strengths."

"When I play my flute, the pigs gather!" Mae said. "That's how I catch them after they escape, if Gelbane isn't watching. I like to pretend it's magick."

Aletta tapped Mae on the nose. "Are you daft? Of course it's magick!"

"What is your strength, Callum?" Mae asked.

"I'm...er, I'm—I'm what you would call a...a Hybilia Frodliker."

"A kitchen witch," Aletta added. She tried to cover up a snorty giggle.

Callum cleared his throat. "It's very rare for a man to be skilled with magick belonging to the home, you know."

Mae smiled and patted Callum's arm consolingly. "You should probably come up with a different name."

Callum cleared his throat. "Hybilia Frodliker is a fine title. We all have weaknesses, too, you know." Callum glared at Aletta. "We'll start to explore yours tomorrow morning, Mae, after a good night's sleep." The wizard pointed down the narrow hallway. "You can take the small room down the hall on the right."

Mae raised her eyebrows. "What do you mean?"

"The cottage will be your home now. You'll stay with Aletta and me and learn to control the magick inside you."

"Stay with you?" She'd never thought about leaving the Wedge, even if she could get away from Gelbane. What if her mother came back to find her gone? Mae reached into her apron pocket. She searched for the comforting feel of the smooth, wooden flute. The raven carving was there, but where was her flute? Her fingers poked into empty corners as her mind played back the journey through the woods. Oh no! She must have dropped the flute when the raven startled her in the barn. "I have to go back," she blurted. "I have to get my mother's flute. I must have dropped it."

Callum and Aletta looked at each other and then at Mae. Aletta gathered Mae's tiny hands in hers. "I can go back and get it for you. Just tell me where it is."

"You...you don't understand," Mae stuttered. "I can't stay here."

"Dear child, of course you can. No more cooking or cleaning for that nasty Gelbane."

"You don't have to be a servant in your own home," Callum added. "You can live with us and learn magick and be free from worry and excessive chores."

Mae took a shuddering breath. "What if my mother comes back, and I'm not there?"

Callum's brows knit together. "It's been six years since she left. Your mother isn't coming back, Maewyn."

"Yes, she is!" Mae crushed her fists together. "Every letter I've ever gotten from her says she's coming back. To not give up!"

"You receive letters from your mother?" Callum asked.

"Yes. Every once in a while, when things get particularly bad with Gelbane, a letter shows up at the doorstep. It's like Momma sends them exactly when I need a boost of hope to keep me going."

Aletta sighed and stood, turning to the wizard. "She isn't ready, Callum. Remy was wrong."

"Remy is never wrong. Maewyn, if you let your magick go untamed, it will likely leave you and choose someone else. Do you understand?"

"Yes," Mae said. "I mean, no. I mean, I understand the words, but I don't understand why I would lose my magick."

"Magick wants to have a master. That's the only way I can explain it." Callum sighed. "I will not force my own wants upon you. You, alone, must make the decision to stay here and learn to control your magick, or return to the Wedge and wait for someone who, in my opinion, will never return. Aletta will show you a shortcut back to the village." Callum turned his chair to the fire and settled into the soft cushions.

Mae nodded and reached for the latch on the door. Her nose twitched and her ears drooped. The door squeaked open, allowing the fragrance of the night to sweep into the room. Aletta trotted past her, having already resumed her pig form.

Mae turned in the doorway. "Thank you, sir."

Callum didn't even turn his head. "No thanks are necessary."

Mae followed Aletta down the steps and over the creek. They trotted through the meadow. The stars were disappearing in the lightening sky as dawn approached.

"Aletta, can you talk when you're a pig?"

"Of course!" she snorted.

"Why didn't you talk to me before?" Mae asked as she and Aletta scrambled underneath a fallen tree.

"Imagine, a pig talking! Most people would run screaming if their livestock talked to them."

Mae brushed her bangs from her face. "I was surprised when Remy called my name. And a little frightened."

"But you were brave to follow him. I was very glad to see you'd made it to our home, and I'm disappointed that you won't stay. You know, I spent some time with your mother before she...went away."

"You knew my mother?"

"She was wonderful. She would scratch my itchy spots and feed me apple peels."

43

"Oh. You knew her as a pig." Mae tried not to let disappointment color her voice.

"Being at the farm is a good way to keep an eye on what is happening in the Wedge without being noticed. We aren't actually allowed in the Wedge, you know. It is some long-ago agreement between the Wizarding world and the hapennies. Callum does a good job with the perimeter, but I wanted a closer look."

"You broke the rules?"

Aletta stopped and turned to Mae. "Sometimes, rules are made to be broken."

"So, you are also a Protector of the Wedge?"

"Not in any official capacity. I'm self-appointed. No dawdling, now. Follow me!" Aletta turned onto a path that led deeper into the woods. The forest was so dense not even a sliver of moonlight managed to filter through the branches. Shadows loomed between trees. Misty tendrils of fog wrapped around trunks. Goose bumps rose on Mae's arms. The hairs on her ears stood alert. "That's not the way I came."

Aletta called over her shoulder, "Callum said to use the shortcut. C'mon!"

Mae wondered if the wizard knew the definition of shortcut, because the path Aletta was taking surely didn't look like one. Mae ran to catch up.

Time seemed to stand still on the dark path. No breeze stirred; no stars blinked. Mae didn't even hear the hoot of an owl. In a few short minutes, she stood at the edge of the Wedge. The river babbled just ahead. To her right, the bridge arched over the rushing water.

"Wow, that was a shortcut!" She patted Aletta's head, forgetting for a moment she wasn't really a pig. "Oh, sorry, Aletta."

"Don't worry about it. We must return you to the barn before Gelbane awakes. I'll help you find your flute, but then I must leave. Unless you've changed your mind?"

"Thank you, Aletta, but I haven't. The farm is my home."

Mae and Aletta ran across the bridge and down the dirt path that led to the farm. Mae yanked the barn door open and toppled into the hay. She tried to remember exactly where she was lying when the raven dropped in. She rolled a sleeping piglet over but had no luck.

Aletta rooted through the hay, brushing it to and fro with her snout and scooching the golden straw with a hoofed toe. "I would change back into my human form, but if Gelbane saw me...well, it's faster to run on four legs."

"That's okay." Mae shoved the boar until he stood up. He wandered over to Aletta and started sniffing her ear.

"Oh, that tickles," Aletta giggled. She bumped the boar with her rump. "Get lost, big guy. I'm not the sow for you."

The boar sauntered to the far corner of the barn and plopped down with an unhappy snort. "Keep looking," Mae said. "Gelbane never wakes this early." She rolled the last piglet over and spotted the brown finish. "Got it!" Mae flopped into the hay with relief. She stretched and yawned. One star still shone faintly in the lightening sky. A blue streak in the sky surprised Mae.

"Look, Aletta!" She pointed to the window high above. "A falling star."

"Quick, make a wish," Aletta said.

There were many things Mae could wish for: cupboards full of her favorite pumpkin bread or a field of golden flax to spin, but only one thing was really important. Mae closed her eyes and wished. She wanted to have magick. She wanted to be a wizard. She wanted to protect the hapennies living in the Wedge. But most of all, she wanted her mother to come home. "Usually I play my flute when I am troubled with wishes. What do you do, Aletta, when you are troubled with wishes?"

"I spend a couple of days as a pig. There's no better remedy than to see the world through someone else's eyes."

"You should go before Gelbane wakes," Mae said. She pulled herself from the warm hay and brushed at the straws clinging to her skirt. "I'll get the door."

Before Mae could reach for the handle, the door burst open.

Gelbane's shadow loomed over Mae. The weak sunlight of early morning silhouetted her form in the doorway. "You don't think you can sneak out in the middle of the night without me noticing, do you?"

"Wha—what do you mean?" Mae stuttered. Her nose twitched at the metallic smell of the iron shackles draped over Gelbane's arm. Her ears flattened against her head and her knees wobbled. The ankle cuffs knocked together with a clang.

"I warned you before." Gelbane knelt and locked the iron cuffs on Mae's ankles, pinching them closed. "Now you'll understand the consequences of sneaking off. I'd like to see you try to run away with those on."

Mae's ears rang as Gelbane's fist caught her in the ear. Tears pooled in her eyes. Bleary-eyed, Mae watched Gelbane saunter across the yard and into the house. The chain connecting her ankles was heavy, and her skin burned under the cuffs. Clouds, like great rolls of grey wool, approached quickly, blocking out the early morning sun. A brisk wind rattled the shingles of the

hen house and slammed the barn door closed. Mae pushed the barn door open slowly, peering into the farmyard.

The wizard trotted behind Mae as she dumped the buckets of slop into the trough for the other pigs and unlatched the door that led to the outside pen.

"Please don't say it," Mae whispered. Her voice cracked with restrained emotion. Her steps were careful and slow as she trudged toward the henhouse. She pulled the door open and wondered if she would be able to get herself up onto the stool in order to reach the eggs she needed to gather.

Aletta's hooves made a soft clicking noise on the wooden floorboards. "I can't do magick when I'm a pig."

"You need to go, Aletta." Mae sniffed. "I'll be fine."

"Are you sure?"

Mae's ears drooped. "I'm sure she'll come back."

"But—"

"No, don't say it, Aletta." She couldn't bear to hear again that her mother wasn't ever coming back.

"Who will help you get out of those chains?"

"I will help myself. You and Callum say I have magick. I might as well learn to use it."

The door creaked open as Aletta pushed against it. "You're sure this is what you want?"

Mae turned away from Aletta's worried expression.

"If you change your mind, just whisper your wish to the forest and Remy will come for you."

Mae nodded and sank to the floor, the burden of her tears weighing her down. She couldn't believe she was giving up the opportunity to get away from Gelbane. The opportunity to protect the hapenny village she loved. The opportunity to be a great wizard.

Chapter Six

A long wooden table, which once shone with polish, was pushed into a corner and piled high with garbage: unwashed bowls, broken cages, and bits of splintery rope. Mae rummaged through the mess for the tinderbox, unable to locate it. She closed her eyes and pictured the box in her mind—the long copper sides and the worn wood top that slid open. A funny feeling tingled in her belly, and Mae suddenly knew she'd find the box in a broken jug under the table. Mae sighed as she searched through Gelbane's discards. She could clean every hour of every day, but not even a hapenny with a fairy godmother could keep up with the mess Gelbane made.

After finding the tinderbox, Mae crawled to the cold hearth. The chain between her ankles clanked over the wood plank floor, scratching the already marred finish. She tossed a handful of dry kindling into the fireplace. Mae struck the flint and steel together until a spark fell onto the tinder. She blew gently until the tinder burst into tiny flames. Then she piled on thicker twigs and waited for them to catch.

Mae ran her hand over the arm of the chair next to the hearth and her throat tightened. The chair reminded her of the wizard. Her stomach grumbled at the remembrance of the feeling of a full belly. Wiping her hands on her apron, Mae listened for Gelbane before standing and trudging into the pantry. The weight of the iron ankle bracelets had lessened a bit over the last few days, but her skin was raw and tender.

She grabbed a cracked porcelain pitcher from the counter and proceeded to the pantry well. Mae pumped the handle, and water trickled out in a steady stream. She stuck the pitcher under it and waited for the stream of water to stop. A sudden crash from Gelbane's workroom made her jump, smashing the pitcher into the iron pipe and chipping off another hunk of porcelain from the rim. "What the day-old-biscuits is she making now?" Mae whispered with irritation. She'd been easily irritated all morning, which was quite unlike her. But Leif had never gone more than two days without visiting. What was keeping him away?

Gathering eggs into her apron, and the pitcher in her hand, Mae made her way back to the hearth. She poured the water into the pot. The eggs made a sploshing noise as she dropped them into the water. She braced her legs and heaved the heavy pot onto the hook over the fire. As she tossed more wood onto the flames, she peered down the hall toward where Gelbane was working. Gelbane seemed to be making more racket than usual, especially for so early in the morning. Mae shuffled as quietly as she could down the hallway, hoping the noise coming from the room would disguise the rattle of the chain.

The door to Gelbane's workroom was ajar, and Mae could see a portion of one of her guardian's contraptions. She strained to see farther into the room. It was jam-packed with machines Gelbane had worked on and discarded over the years.

Things whirled and bounced and whistled. Something ticked; glass tubes vibrated with boiling liquid the color of ginger beer. What looked like a rusty wire cage was half hidden in the corner. She craned her neck to see in further and bumped the door.

"You know you aren't supposed to be snooping in my workroom!" Gelbane instantly filled the space like a curtain drawn over a window. Her guardian snapped the door closed, but not before Mae caught a glimpse of something cowering in the cage.

"I wasn't 'snooping,'" Mae said.

"Wasn't snooping? What would you call it, then?"

"I was just coming to tell you—" Mae wrung her hands and her mind raced. "That...that breakfast is ready."

"Good, I'm starving." Gelbane turned the key in the door, locking it fast. "In fact, I'm so hungry, I think I'll eat your portion." Gelbane sniggered wickedly as she pushed Mae aside and squashed past her in the narrow hall, turning into Mae's mother's room, which Gelbane had taken over just a few days after Mae's mother had left.

Mae glanced at the workroom door. Gelbane was keeping something in that cage, and she had a powerful urge to find out what it was.

Gelbane poked her head back into the hallway. "Move it, you lazy wretch!"

Mae shuffled past her guardian, through the parlor, and into the pantry. What kind of creature was Gelbane keeping in that cage?

Her fingers shook as she sliced a leftover biscuit in half, catching her fingertip with the knife's sharp edge. The cut stung and Mae wrapped her injured finger in her apron to stop the trickle of blood that oozed out. With her other hand she stacked the biscuits on a chipped plate, balanced the knife on the edge, and carried everything to the table in the parlor.

The fire glinted off the knife blade and made it glow a strange green color. Mae blinked and shook her head. She must be very tired. That or her magick was acting up. She was trying to master it, as Callum had said, but odd things were still happening. At least the pigs hadn't escaped in a couple of days. Setting the plate on the table, she scooped a spoon into the boiling water and fished out the cooked eggs.

Mae held her finger up by the firelight. Her finger was wrinkled like when she spent too much time in the tub, but at least the bleeding had stopped. It was just a small cut, but day-old-biscuits, did it sting!

After peeling off the shells, she sliced an egg and almost choked when she saw the yolk. It was purple, like an oval amethyst nestled in a bed of cotton. She placed the white egg slices in between the biscuits and shoved the yolks in her mouth, hoping Gelbane wouldn't notice.

Mae scurried to the pantry and washed the yolk down with a gulp of water from the pump. Gelbane was sitting at the table when Mae stepped back into the room, just in time to see her guardian snatch a cricket from under the mess of garbage and bite down with a loud crunch. Mae stopped cold. Her stomach rolled. The egg yolks bubbled and threatened to come spewing back up. She'd never seen a hapenny eat an insect before.

Gelbane sneered. Her eyes narrowed and she bared her teeth. "Shut your gob, afore I shut it for you!" Her fist slammed on the table, making the broken bits and bobs dance.

Mae set the cup on the table and snapped her jaws shut.

Curling a fist at Mae, Gelbane growled, "If you have time for snooping and ogling me, maybe you need some more chores to keep you busy."

Mae shuffled from the room and back into the pantry. More chores! She already swept the chimneys and scrubbed the floors, mucked the stalls and cut the hay, tended the garden, fed the animals and did all the cooking. Callum and Aletta were right; she was a servant in her own home. She'd waited for six long years for her mother to return and all she'd received were vague letters telling her to be good for Gelbane. Well, she was tired of being good for Gelbane. She would go back to Callum as soon as she could, even if she had to drag the chain all the way through the forest.

Mae peered around the arch that separated the two rooms, anxiously bouncing up and down on her toes, waiting for Gelbane finish her breakfast. Now that she'd decided to leave, she couldn't wait for the chance to do so.

Finally, Gelbane lifted the biscuit to her mouth. She gnashed at the bread with her yellowed teeth. She bent forward to take another bite and paused. Peeling the top half of the biscuit off, her face turned scarlet. She lifted her nose like a hunting dog and sniffed, nostrils flaring. "What's that smell? What's that smell?" She dropped the biscuit like a hot potato and pounded the tabletop with her meaty fist.

"It smells like blood! You careless, undersized, not even a mouthful of hairy fluff!" Gelbane rose, sending the chair cartwheeling across the room. "You think I won't notice that you've bled all over my breakfast?"

Mae held up her finger. "It was just a tiny cut. Didn't hardly bleed at all."

"'Didn't hardly bleed at all!'" Gelbane mocked. She stuck her nose in the air and sniffed again, stalking toward Mae.

Mae stumbled back.

"How can I eat eggs when all I can think about is the smell of your blood?" The glint in her eyes held a sharp edge.

It took all of Mae's strength to scramble onto the countertop, dragging the weight of the iron ankle cuffs and chain with her. Her guardian's heavy breathing roared into the pantry.

"Leave me alone!" Mae yelled as she struggled to pull open the pantry window.

Gelbane caught the chain and pulled. It snapped, releasing Mae from its constraint and flinging Gelbane backwards. Mae clung to the sill with one hand and tried to pull the window open with the other. Finally it came loose, groaning and creaking as Mae yanked it open. She struggled to pull herself through the window, grateful, for once, to be the smallest hapenny in the Wedge. She felt the ribbon on her necklace give way as her chest slid over the wooden sill.

Gelbane's sharp nails raked down Mae's calf and pressed into her ankle. Welts formed and blood beaded up. Her foot throbbed. Mae struggled and kicked her legs, catching her captor's nose with her heel. She saw Gelbane's eyes fill with tears and took the split-second advantage she'd fought to win. She booted Gelbane again, catching her in the chin, and her guardian released her grasp, hands cupping her bleeding nose.

Mae hauled herself onto the grass and hobbled toward the forest, grimacing with each step. A door slammed and Gelbane bellowed, "I'll find you, you little pest! I'll find you and chain you to the hearth this time so you can't run away!"

Mae's head swam, and her vision blurred as she reached the bridge. The forest looked like an oil painting, all big swirls of color and no detail. She fell to her hands and knees as the world turned around her. "You can't stop now," Mae said to herself, trying to pluck up her courage. "She's bound to follow."

Aletta's voice echoed in her head. *Whisper your wish to the forest...*

A warm, wet nose poked her in the face.

So much for learning to master her magick. The pigs had escaped again. But maybe she could use that to her advantage.

Mae reached out to the pig and struggled to drag herself over its back.

The sharp sound of snapping twigs echoed behind her. Heavy footsteps resonated through the wood. Gelbane!

Mae wound her arms around the pig's bristly neck, and the animal trotted off into the forest. Gelbane's furious howl echoed off the trunks of the trees. The clouds that had threatened all morning chose that moment to release raindrops the size of toadstools.

Shooting pain radiated up Mae's leg with every bounce of the pig's gait. She couldn't really make sense of anything. Her blood raced through her ears like the wind through the hollow. Her limbs felt like they were stuffed with chicken feathers. She flattened her ears against her head and whispered to the pig, "Take me to Callum's cottage in the wood. And may the wind give you wings."

Chapter Seven

Water splashed Mae's feet as the pig dashed through the creek in front of Callum's cottage. The animal's paced slowed, and Mae slipped from its back to become a shivering mass on the ground. She could do nothing but curl into a miserable ball in the grass. A weak moan vibrated in her throat.

Quick footsteps *shushed* across the cobblestones, and strong arms plucked her from the ground. The smell of peppermint and fresh bread clung to Callum. The long hairs of his beard tickled her face, but Mae had no energy to swipe them away.

"What happened?" Callum asked, his voice rough and whispery.

"I don't know. I found her at the edge of the forest." Aletta transformed out of her pigskin.

"She is lucky you were near." Callum climbed the steps to the cottage and laid Mae in the overstuffed chair. Remy cawed and shifted above her.

Callum's hand settled on the iron cuffs around her ankles. "Why didn't you tell me?" he asked Aletta.

Aletta shrugged. "What good would it have done?"

"We could have helped her!"

"She didn't want our help, Callum."

Callum scoffed and muttered, and Mae felt the weight of the iron cuffs fall away from her ankles. She looked down at her legs. The wounds on her calf were crusting up with a foul green tinge. The crust and discoloration made her feel a little woozy. Her head swam; the room swirled. She closed her eyes and concentrated on the crackling fire. The room seemed overly warm. She pulled at the neck of her dress. Sweat beaded on her brow.

"What can I do to help?" Aletta paced back and forth. Anxiety oozed from her voice.

Callum's cool hand pressed against Mae's heel. "Get me the jar of balm, with the green ribbon and the gold seal in the shape of a leaf, from the pantry."

Something tickled Mae's arm like the brush of Mr. Blackburrow's cat's whiskers did when he curled around her ankles. Mae opened her eyes a bit. The fancy-dressed critters she'd seen on her first visit looked at her from the arm of the chair. Their whiskers shivered like the strings of a lute just plucked. Their tails quivered with nervous energy.

"Beau, Trina," Callum said, "I know you are worried about Maewyn, but she might find it a little unnerving for you to be staring at her. Make yourselves useful and find some bandages."

The red squirrels scurried down the chair, their tiny nails making *scritch-scratch* noises against the fabric. Aletta swept back into the room, carrying a jar. Callum popped the lid on the ointment and a bitter smell filled Mae's nostrils.

She crinkled her nose at the stench.

"I know it smells worse than the largest pile of ogre poo, but it is the best thing for a..." Callum cleared his throat. "For a wound of this type."

The balm was cool on Mae's skin; it felt good despite the fact that it smelled horrid. Beau and Trina hurried across the room, rolls of linen strips unwinding behind them.

Mae tried to sit up, but dizziness overtook her again. She curled up in the chair, reaching into her pocket and running her thumb over the flute's soft grain for comfort. Mae closed her eyes as she waited for the world to settle.

"Can you tell me what happened, Maewyn?"

"I tried to learn to master my magick, honestly I did, but the yolks were purple, so I ate them. And I cut my finger slicing the eggs. Gelbane said I ruined her breakfast with my blood." Mae opened her eyes and held her injured finger up. "It was just a small cut. It hardly bled at all. Then she lunged at me and I escaped through the pantry window. She tried to stop me."

Squinting at the tiny digit, Callum pointed to the green tinge that was spreading on Mae's wrinkled finger. "It seems you are going to need some ointment on that as well."

"She made me lose my necklace, too," Mae pouted. "I should've listened to you. I should've never gone back!"

"We will get your necklace," Aletta said. "Please don't worry yourself into a tizzy. You'll need your strength to heal."

Callum was very gentle about wrapping her injuries, and Mae's eyes drooped with weariness. Trina crept toward her, whiskers shivering, and Mae reached out to the squirrel, rubbing the soft fur under her chin. "Your dress is very pretty, Trina." Delicate white lace trimmed the cuffs.

Trina's nose twitched and she curled the end of her tail, eyes lighting up.

Mae had outgrown her nice dresses three and a half years ago. Gelbane didn't think they needed to be replaced. She told Mae that a good bucket and a sturdy shovel, not nice dresses, were all she needed to slop the pigs and shovel manure.

"Maewyn," Aletta knelt in front of her, "the knife that you cut your finger on, can you tell us what it looked like?"

Mae shrugged. "It was just a regular old kitchen knife."

"Did it have a special pattern on it?"

"No, but..."

"But?" Aletta's eyes bored into hers.

"When I took the knife into the sitting room, the blade reflected the firelight, but the reflection was green, not orange or red, not even yellow. I blinked and the green was gone. I thought I was just tired or that my magick was acting up."

Aletta gasped. "It is as I feared!"

"Now, now, Aletta, let's not be melodramatic. You'll frighten the poor girl."

Mae chewed on her lip. "Is there something wrong?"

Callum ran his hand over her mud-brown curls, brushing her long bangs off her forehead. "It is nothing you need to worry about right now. Let's give your injuries some time to heal, and then we will talk about Aletta's suspicions." He turned to Aletta, who had risen from Mae's side and was pacing by the

hearth, chewing on a thumbnail. "And that's all they are right now: suspicions."

"But—"

Callum held up a hand. "We will talk about this later."

Mae wanted to know what Aletta was worried about, but she didn't have the strength to argue with the wizard. Callum went about preparing a cup of tea, and Mae was grateful when he handed it to her. "Do you think you'll be able to keep this down?"

"I'm a hapenny." Mae attempted to smile. "I can eat more in one meal than a nest of baby birds."

"Yes." Callum grinned back at her. "I almost forgot."

The tea soothed her weary, injured body. Mae's eyelids drooped. She sniffed the last dregs. "What's in this? Lavender?" she asked with a yawn.

"Yes, some of that and more of something else, to help you heal and sleep." Callum tucked a frayed blanket around her. He took the cup as her eyes closed. Her ears tried to perk up again as Aletta whispered in a husky voice, but Mae caught only one word.

Troll.

"She said the knife glinted green, Callum. And the state of the house—it wasn't tidy, not like a hapenny's house should be."

Chapter Eight

"And you've never noticed this before?"

"I was a pig! I've never been in the house! I only peeked in the windows today because I was checking in on Mae."

Mae opened her eyes. She was not in the chair by the fire anymore, but in a large bed, the frayed blanket tucked around her. Aletta and Callum argued as they walked down the hallway, pausing in front of her door. Mae closed her eyes again and pretended to be asleep. The flute in her pocket vibrated against her leg.

"Maybe Gelbane is just disorganized."

Aletta clicked her tongue. "Have you ever heard of a messy hapenny? Or one with such a bad temper?"

"Have you ever heard of a hapenny wizard?" Callum retorted.

"It isn't the same, Callum, and you know it! What about the knife? What about the missing boys? And the scratches on Maewyn's leg? Those didn't come from fingernails!"

"You're right; there is strong proof, but taking action before there is reason can be dangerous as well."

Strains of music floated through the room. Mae sat up, forgetting about playing opossum, and pulled the flute from her pocket. She held the little instrument in her hand as it played. Aletta and Callum walked through her doorway.

"Has it ever done that before?" Callum asked. His eyes were as big as saucers.

Mae shook her head.

Callum held out his hand. "May I see it?"

She gave the flute to Callum. The man held it up to the firelight and shook his head. "Amazing. I don't see anything to suggest an enchantment, besides the fact that it plays by itself."

Aletta bent to peer at the singing instrument. "It sounds like a song I've heard before." She hummed a few bars. "I've heard the village children sing it when they play a little game. It teaches them about the pox."

"How clever." Callum rubbed his chin. "Education in a nursery rhyme. I've always said non-magickal peoples are underestimated."

The song sparked a memory in Mae's head, too, and she remembered something about bridges, and hapennies rolling carts. Mae got a feeling that the flute was trying to send her a message. If only she could remember the words. The music faded and stopped. The air in the room tingled with anticipation.

Callum handed the flute back to Mae and she put it in her pocket, the melody still spinning in her mind. "I heard you arguing," she mumbled.

"We were only having a discussion." Aletta sat beside her and patted her hand.

The two faces in front of Mae were both etched with worry. "It sounded more like an argument to me," she said, looking from one wizard to the other. "What boys are missing?"

Aletta exchanged a glance with Callum. He shook his head. "It's nothing you need to worry about right now. You need to concentrate on getting well."

Mae's stomach growled. It seemed to her it had been quite a while since she had last eaten. "Did I miss breakfast?" She wanted to get her strength back quickly, and nothing was better for strength than a big plate of blueberry pancakes.

Callum chuckled. "Yes, and noon meal. Aletta worried that I put too much sleeping herb in your tea."

"I still think he did!" Aletta patted Mae's leg and rose from the bed. "I'll see what I can find in the pantry for you."

"My ankle feels much better already." Mae pushed the blanket from her lap and stuck out her leg. "Can I learn some magick today?"

"Let's take a look." Callum bent to unwrap the bandage. The wound had sealed itself, and only a bit of the ghoulish green color remained. He held her hand up to the light coming through the window. A small, brown scab had formed over the cut on her finger, too. Callum clicked his tongue and sighed. "Well, I still think another day of rest wouldn't hurt."

Mae stuck out her lower lip. "Hapennies are not suited to idleness."

Callum's eyes sparkled with amusement. "You need plenty of rest to heal properly. A short walk in the forest and then an afternoon nap should do the trick."

"I don't need a nap! I'm not a newlyborn!"

"All right, I'll let you read instead of insisting that you sleep. But if you happen to fall asleep, it's not my fault. How's that?"

Mae scowled.

"Or I could give you some more tea," Callum suggested.

"No, reading is fine! Better than a nap, anyway." Mae did not want to sleep any more of the day away. Her eyes scanned a pile of books in the corner. She pointed to a red, clothbound book. The title was scrawled across the spine in faded gold letters: A Historie of Magickal Peoples. "Can I start with that one?"

Aletta returned and placed a plate loaded with cheese, bread, tender spring greens, and a bit of roasted fowl on the dresser next to the bed. Callum pulled the red book from the pile and brushed the dust from its cover. "Yes, this would be a great start to your magickal education."

"Magickal education?"

Callum's eyebrows rose over the brim of his hat. "You didn't think we would just turn you loose with all that magick inside, did you?"

Mae shrugged. She hadn't been to school since her momma went away. Mrs. Fairstone, the village schoolteacher, had pleaded with Gelbane to let Mae return with the other students, but Gelbane had gnashed her teeth and growled at the meek woman to mind her place. Gelbane had said that she was Mae's guardian, as requested by her mother should anything dreadful happen to her, and she would do what she thought was best for Mae.

"Now, when you are finished eating, get dressed and join me in the hearth room." Callum placed the book at the foot of her bed. "A little walk should loosen up those sore muscles."

"What about trolls?"

"Trolls?"

Mae nodded as she scarfed down some cheese and bits of meat.

"The sun is shining very brightly; we won't have to worry about those beasts today." Callum hummed as he left her to eat her mid-afternoon feast.

As Mae ate, her eyes scoured the room. It was tidy, and the walls were painted a soft color that reminded Mae of robins' eggs. Under a row of windows, a second bed sat against the wall. A green cover was tucked in tightly at the corners, and a white skirting flowed around the iron frame. Hanging on a hook by the door was a cotton dress and a perfect white pinafore (with pockets!). At the foot of the bed, next to the book, were striped leggings and a pair of lace-up leather boots.

After pulling the dress and pinafore from the hook, Aletta held it up for Mae's inspection. "Callum made this for you last night. It's very pretty, isn't it?"

"Blue is my favorite color," Mae said. "But the best part is, it's clean!"

Aletta laughed. "Yes, you would see it that way, wouldn't you?"

Mae grinned. "The lace is very pretty."

"I thought I saw you fingering Trina's cuffs yesterday." Aletta laid the pleated pinafore on the mattress.

Mae crawled to the end of the bed and flopped on her rear. The mattress barely dented from her little weight. She pulled the leggings on, one foot at a time. Her ankle was still a bit painful, but she gritted her teeth against the short-lived twinge. No way was she staying in bed one more moment than she must. The leggings of blue, green, and yellow stripes were made from a thick material. She wiggled her toes against their softness. They would block the spring breeze and keep her warm.

She pulled her dirty dress over her head and tossed it on the floor. In an instant, it disappeared. With alarm, Mae pointed to the floor. "Where did it go? My flute was in the pocket! And my raven!"

"That's one of Callum's spells." Aletta handed her the clean dress. "Your flute and raven are now in the pinafore pocket, and your dress will be back, cleaned, mended, and hung on the hook, by tomorrow morning."

"Imagine never having to clean again, but everything still being tidy, just the way a hapenny likes it," Mae said as she slipped her head and arms into the bodice. "I've changed my mind. I'd rather be a kitchen witch instead of learning how to transform into an animal."

"They both have advantages, I suppose." Aletta straightened the straps of the pinafore on Mae's shoulders and reached for the boots. As Aletta loosened the bootlaces, Mae slipped her hand into her pocket, just to make sure. The flute was there, tucked into the corner, the raven right next to it. Mae pulled a boot on her injured ankle carefully and reached for the next. Then, turning on her belly, she held onto the bed sheets as she slipped down to the floor. Immediately her bootlaces tightened and the pinafore was a little too snug around her waist. "Another of Callum's spells?" she asked.

"You've got it." Aletta smiled. "That color is most becoming. Shall we join Callum in the hearth room?"

"Can you loosen the bow on my apron first? I feel like I can't breathe!"

Aletta laughed and loosened the bow, and then Mae tested her injured ankle. The boots were tall and helped to support her ankle. She wiggled her toes inside the stiff leather. After being so free for so long, her toes felt a little smothered. She smiled up at her new friend. "Callum uses the braided end of his beard like a wand. Do you have a wand, Aletta?"

The wizard shook her sleeve and a thin tendril of grapevine appeared in her hand.

Mae stared at it in disbelief. "I would have expected it to be a little bigger."

Aletta poked her wand back into her sleeve. "Yes, well, you'll see. It's not as if I chose a grapevine wand."

As she padded down the hallway behind the wizard, Mae wondered at how this could be true. Why didn't Aletta choose her own wand? A wand seemed to be a most personal thing.

Callum was at his worktable when she and Aletta entered the room. Mae pulled nervously at the hem of her pinafore.

Callum clapped his hands together. "How marvelous you look, Maewyn! I'm glad I decided on stripes instead of polka dots. They suit you."

"Thank you for the dress and apron and tights. The stripes are wonderful, although polka dots would have been nice, too."

Callum laughed. "Next time, polka dots, then!"

"Next time?" Mae asked.

"I'm sorry, I assumed after Gelbane attacked you...uh... You will be staying with us for good now, won't you, Maewyn?"

Mae nodded. She wouldn't be Gelbane's servant ever again. She couldn't really go back, anyway, not after she had kicked her guardian in the face and run away. "Could I please send Leif a letter, though, so he won't worry about me?"

Callum and Aletta exchanged glances.

"I won't tell him where I am, I mean, if you don't want me to." Mae dropped her gaze to the floor and twisted the corner of her apron. "Just that I'm safe and that one day soon I'll come back to the Wedge."

Callum cleared his throat. "It's not that we don't want you to tell Leif where you are, it's just that we would fear for your safety if Gelbane found out."

Aletta pulled a woolen cloak across her shoulders. "I'm going to be gone for a few days. If you write that letter, I'll make sure it gets delivered when I return."

"Where are you going?" Mae asked. She had been looking forward to getting to know Aletta better.

The wizards exchanged another glance. They seemed to be doing that a lot today.

"I'm going to be spending a few days at the farm. I need to play the pig a while longer."

"But why?" Mae cried. Her heartbeat picked up speed as fear gushed through her body.

"Call it a fondness for slops." Aletta's smile wavered around the edges. "I'll be just fine. I've handled Gelbane before. Don't worry. I'll be back by the time you finish that book sitting on your bed."

"Let's walk Aletta out, shall we, Mae?"

Callum pulled the front door open and followed the two onto the porch. "Take care, Aletta."

Aletta stretched to peck Callum on the forehead and pinched Mae's cheeks. They watched from the porch until she disappeared into the woods. Then Callum held out his hand to Mae. "Shall we begin?"

Mae nodded and curled her hand around Callum's finger. She knew he was trying to distract her, but she couldn't help worrying about Aletta. She hoped Gelbane didn't catch her and decide that runaway pigs should be eaten.

Chapter Nine

The birds flittered to and fro, anxious to put the finishing touches on their nests as Mae and Callum picked their way across the creek on the stepping-stones. The squirrels called to each other, sharing stories about tender spring shoots and nut stores. The sun shone through the trees' spring leaves and dappled the trunks with spots of bright light.

Mae considered each step. She didn't want to trip and injure her ankle more, or Callum would make her wait even longer to learn a bit of magick. The wizard was just ahead of her. Every once in a while he would stop, put his hand to his chin and look very thoughtful.

During one of those moments, Mae crawled atop a low tree stump and plopped down. "Are we lost, Callum?"

"What?" The man turned to her. "Oh, no, no. We aren't lost, exactly; I have merely turned myself around a bit. You rest while I find the right path." Callum peered into the forest and, settling his cap further back on his head, disappeared behind a thicket of trees.

Mae rolled her achy ankle; it was tender, even with the extra support of the ankle-high boot. Swiveling on her perch, Mae peered past the underbrush. A meadow lay just beyond her seat on the tree stump. When they were younger, she had often wandered with Leif to a small meadow to pick flowers, with his little brother, Reed, in tow. Reed still shadowed his older brother almost everywhere.

The sun lit upon the flowers in the meadow, painting them a golden hue. A lone tree grew in the center. Its leaves were shaped like feathers, and creamy white buds burst forth from the ends of the branches.

Mae pointed to the tree and yelled to Callum, "What kind of tree is that?"

But the wizard had moved too far away to hear, so Mae slipped from the stump and made her way through the underbrush. When she reached the tree, she ran her hand over the smooth bark and touched the fuzzy buds.

Reaching down with a twiggy finger, the tree snagged Mae's hair.

"Hey!" Mae yelped, rubbing her head. She felt a tug at the bow of her pinafore. Mae turned in a circle, trying to catch the ends of her ties. "That wasn't very nice!"

She pulled the flute out of her pocket and stepped back from the grabbing fingers. Mae licked her lips and then put the flute to them. A soft tune, like a gentle wind meandering through the forest, mingled with the breeze.

The tree bent and swayed to the beat. Mae stared as the buds on the limbs unfurled into creamy white flowers. The center of each blossom formed a yellow star. Then the tree flung out a slender sprig, which landed at Mae's feet. She bent to pick it up, the flute's song fading into the forest.

Callum entered the meadow. "I should have known you two would be a perfect match. Luisliu is a mischievous tree."

The leaves on the tree shook, as if it was laughing.

Mae pocketed the flute, then twirled the twig in her hand, inspecting the velvety star centers of the flowers. "Luisliu?"

"That's the name of the tree, Luisliu. I think non-magickal people call it a rowan tree. In the fall, it will be covered with beautiful red berries." Callum patted his stomach. "The berries make a wonderful jam."

Mae's mouth watered at the idea of making jam. She swallowed and gazed up into the tree's swaying canopy. "Sounds wonderful."

"It is particularly good with goose." The wizard chuckled. "It makes perfect sense that your wand would come from this tree."

Mae blinked and stared at the sprig in her hand. "My wand?"

Callum unbraided the end of his beard, revealing a thorny twig of raspberry. "No other wizard I've ever met has a thorn-riddled wand. But it entangled itself around my leg, and I knew that it was meant to be."

Mae smiled and gripped the twig tighter. "My wand!"

A breeze picked up as Mae hobbled back to the tree. She threw her arms around its trunk. "Thank you, Luisliu." She patted the smooth bark.

Callum braided his wand back into his beard, and then put his hand on the top of Mae's head. "Come, Maewyn, it feels like there's a storm blowing in, and it's time for you to rest."

"But I'm too excited to rest! I want to learn some magick!" She turned in a circle and gave the wand a flick with her wrist. "Kazoo!" The flowers burst off the twig, turning into white moths that fluttered to and fro.

"Oh, dear." Callum's mouth quirked to the side. "It seems I've underestimated your magick. No more wand flicking until I can teach you some rules, or I fear you will be turning mushrooms into hobgoblins." Callum turned away from the meadow. "Come along, Maewyn."

Mae followed the wizard, but when she saw a ring of polka-dotted toadstools, she couldn't resist. With a picture in her mind of what she thought hobgoblins looked like and a little flick of her wrist, Mae tapped each toadstool with her wand. At first nothing happened. And then, one by one, the toadstools sprouted legs and scurried away. Mae was so startled she ran to catch up with Callum, ignoring the twinge in her ankle. She grabbed his shirttail and looked back. A cluster of little creatures with round features and gleaming eyes stared at her from the brush. On their heads, bulbous red hats with white polka dots bounced with excitement. The hobgoblins were just as she'd pictured them. She waved as Callum pulled her along, hoping they would follow her, but they scurried deeper into the woods. She hoped she'd see them again and that they would be able to keep dry in the storm. She supposed, though, that a toadstool had weathered many spring showers. A splash of rain fell on her nose, and the wizard picked up his pace.

Callum and Mae made it to the shelter of the porch as the storm began in earnest. Mae wasn't about to admit it, but she was a little tired. She rested in the bed in the room that was now hers. It wasn't her dreaming nook, but it was cozy enough. A half-drained cup of tea and three biscuits were sitting on a plate next to her. Her new wand rested on the table by the bed.

She reached for the wand and twirled it in her hand, this time being very careful to stop any images from forming in her mind. "Callum, should I whittle the bumps down on my wand?"

"Oh, no." The wizard shook his head. "You must never use metal on a rowan tree or you will hurt its magick. The bumps will smooth in time from use."

Callum picked up the large tome at the end of her bed and settled the heavy book in Mae's lap. "Knowing about the past helps us avoid mistakes in the future."

Placing her wand by her side, Mae flipped open the cover of A Historie of Magickal People. Some of the pages had corners worn from the many fingers turning them through the years. She ran her hand over the yellowed paper, soft with age, and then she began to read.

Chapter Ten

The storm pounded the Wedge for two days and nights, plenty of time for Mae to worry about Aletta, who still hadn't returned.

She'd been reading, too, moving on from the Historie of Magickal People to Bits and Baubles for Beginners. The soft crackle in the hearth was a nice accompaniment to the rain drumming against the roof.

Callum was tying fishing flies. Downy black feathers were stuck to his beard. Mae heard him muttering curses under his breath more than once at the tangled red thread. With a big sigh, Callum put the flies aside and put another log on the fire. He glanced at the door and sighed again. The wizard hadn't said so, but Mae was sure he was worried, too.

Mae wiggled in the small, overstuffed chair Callum had magicked for her and snapped her book closed. Trina startled and unwound from her nest in Mae's curls where she had taken up residence. She climbed down to Mae's shoulder, her whiskers tickling the girl's neck. Mae gathered the squirrel in her hands and set Trina on the arm of the chair. "Callum, can

you tell me what it feels like to change shape? Does it hurt?"
She hadn't only been worried about Aletta; she'd been worried
about the toadstools turned into hobgoblins, too.

The wizard sank into his chair before the fire. He rubbed
his hands over his eyes. "It doesn't hurt, exactly...and Aletta
says you get used to it. She once explained the feeling as a bit
like the popping sensation when your knuckles crack."

"It would be awfully useful to be able to change into
something different than a hapenny." Mae peeked at Callum
through her eyelashes.

"Aletta has called Verdan Gripora useful as well, but she's not especially fond of her magickal strength." He chuckled, lost in thought for a moment. "I suppose she would feel differently if she transformed into a nobler creature."

Mae shrugged her shoulders. "I like pigs. Do you think Aletta will teach me?"

Callum rubbed his whiskery chin. "I don't know, Maewyn; it's tough magick. Perhaps we should stick to the more basic spells for now." Callum tapped his finger on the end of his nose. Mae bit her lip with anticipation. She turned her ears forward and made her eyes as round as possible.

The wizard sighed and smiled. "How can I say no with you looking at me like that?" A belly laugh rippled through the cottage. "I guess it won't hurt to see if you have a tendency toward a Verdan Gripora or a Kiptar Liftan. It does seem to fit with the blossoms turning into moths and such." Callum clapped his hand on the arm of the chair. "You're feeling well enough for this?"

Mae nodded. Her stomach flip-flopped with excitement... or maybe it was hunger. Breakfast had been quite a while ago.

Callum pointed to the kindling pile. "Hand me that twig there."

Mae jumped from her seat—her ankle didn't even twinge today—and pulled the stick out of the pile. She handed it to the wizard.

He held it up in the firelight. "What does it look like to you?"

Mae raised her eyebrows skeptically. "It's a twig."

Shaking his head, Callum clicked his tongue. "No, I asked what it looks like, not what it is."

Mae scanned the dips and swells of the bark on the twig. At first the twig looked like an ordinary twig, but then she

found a couple of bumps and a little knothole. If she let her imagination go free, she could almost see the face of a weasel, the bumps being brow ridges and the knothole a cute, black nose.

The twig twinged in Callum's grasp. "Yes, that's it," he whispered. "Now use your wand."

Mae pulled her wand from her apron pocket and settled the tip on the twig. Two beady eyes stared out from the rough surface, blinking at the firelight.

A furry paw swiped at the knothole nose. One end of the twig waved like a tail.

Trina scampered up the wizard's arm and hid in the brim of his hat, where Beau was watching with wary eyes and shivering whiskers.

The front door jolted in its casing and then blew open. The weasel squirmed from Callum's grip and scrambled up the bookshelves.

Aletta swept in on the rain-laden wind. The raven followed, gliding to the top of Callum's chair. The stormy entrance of her two friends made Mae forget about the weasel. Aletta's usually neat hair was frizzy and sticking out from under her hat in every direction. The tail of her cap drooped sadly to the ground.

"What we need," Aletta announced, "is a weather wizard!" She seized her hat and flipped it onto a peg behind the door. "I don't suppose Mae is one of those?"

The wizard wrung her hair in the doorway and snapped her fingers at the mop in the corner. The mop sprang to life and sopped up the rain from the entryway, then went after the dripping woman.

"No, no!" Aletta said in a singsong voice. "Go away, you twig-brained mop!"

Mae giggled as Aletta shooed the mop away and latched the front door. She was relieved Aletta had finally returned.

Callum gestured to the weasel peering out at them from the bookshelves. "We were just doing a little test. Seems our Maewyn has many talents. Though Vedar Frodliker, or a weather wizard as you so plainly put it, doesn't seem to be one of them. Kiptar Liftan, however, may be on the top of the list."

"That's a wizard that can bring something to life," Mae said. She cringed at the thought of the toadstool creatures running around the forest. Had they found shelter from the storm? She hadn't thought about that when she'd left them behind. "I read about some famous Kiptar Liftans in A Historie of Magickal People." She patted the red book in her chair. "I didn't read about any Hybilia Frodlikers in the book though, Callum."

Red splotches grew on Callum's cheeks. "That's because Hybilia Frodlikers rarely do anything noteworthy."

Aletta kissed the tip of his nose and ruffled his hair on her way to the hearth. "I wouldn't give up yet, my pet." The sopping hem of her dress left a wet trail behind her, like one a snail leaves on a rock.

"We were getting worried about you," Callum grumbled. "Did you run into trouble?"

"Well, Gelbane managed to corral the pigs back up in the barn, poor things. The chickens, however, are loose and roosting in the trees at the edge of the forest." Aletta turned and frowned. The dark smudges under her sunken eyes told Mae she had not rested well during her foray into the Wedge.

"Did you happen to hear if Mother Underknoll has been found yet?" Mae asked hopefully.

The wizard held her hands out to the fire and shook her head. "I'm sorry, Mae. There's been no news of her."

Aletta took a deep breath. "I did hear Ms. Gnarlroot is taking care of the newlyborn for Mr. Underknoll until Mother Underknoll can be found. Many in the Wedge are worried..."

"And?" Mae asked.

"And..." Aletta hesitated. "The Burrbridge brothers were sent to the market a few days ago, the day we first met you, I believe, and they never returned."

Mae bolted to her feet and stomped to the window. "Now Leif is missing? I have to find him!" She stared out the window, nose pressing against the cold glass pane. The petals of the night-blooming flowers were pulled closed against the wind and blowing rain. Farther off, the creek, now full to bursting over its bed, rushed by. Sorrow and worry found a place to settle in her chest, like a bird roosting in a bush. She turned to face the wizards. "Something isn't right. That's three hapennies missing: first Mother Underknoll and now Leif and Reed."

"I'm sure it is just coincidence," Callum said.

A shadow passed through Aletta's eyes. Mae was sure Aletta wasn't convinced that the disappearances were coincidence. And neither was she.

Mae let out a keening wail. The weasel jumped from the bookshelf to the floor and slunk under Callum's chair. Aletta rushed to her side. "Not many creatures will be wandering around in a storm like this," Aletta said, trying to console her. "Hopefully that will mean no more disappearances. We know you are anxious to help your friend, his brother, and Mother Underknoll. But more than likely, we are dealing with some very dark magick, and we want you to be safe." The wizard smoothed Mae's hair from her face. "We should eat and form a plan of action. That will make you feel better, won't it? I'm starving. You must be hungry, too."

Mae took a calming breath. "Leif always says it is better to form a plan on a full stomach."

"That's my girl." Callum grabbed the end of his beard and gave his wand a twirl. On the small table next to his chair a plate appeared piled high with cheese, round slices of sausage, and some chunks of warm bread. Garnishing the plate was a clump of plum-colored grapes. Three cups of tea appeared on shiny copper saucers.

Mae eyed the tea suspiciously.

"It's not sleeping tea, Maewyn," Aletta said. "Dig in."

Callum sighed. "The Wedge is right to be worried. There haven't been any disappearances since the Great Invasion."

The flute trembled in Mae's pocket. "The Great Invasion?"

"Remember I told you that knowing about the past helps us avoid mistakes in the future? The Great Invasion was a time of great concern in the Wedge. Hapennies were disappearing," Callum said.

"Just like now," Aletta added. "The hapennies banded together and caught the troll responsible. Unfortunately, many were lost."

"The Great Protector, Remington Gythal, helped guard the people of the Wedge from another troll attack by putting a spell on the bridge," Mae said. "I read about him. No trolls can cross the bridge or they will change into stone."

"That's right." Callum reached up to stroke the raven. "I was his apprentice when I was young. It seems many trolls have attempted to cross the bridge, from the stones I've had to clear away when I patrol the borders." Callum pointed to his head. "Some of them are lacking in wit."

"Perhaps." Aletta sat on the hearth. "But when you are a pig, you've got a lot of time to think. What if the trolls aren't as dim-witted as we presume? What if they have found a way around the spell?"

Mae startled as her flute burst forth in urgent sound. She snatched it from her pocket. "I think my flute is trying to tell us something!"

The flute twittered happily.

Aletta's eyes widened. "I think you are right."

Plopping next to the wizard, Mae propped her elbows on her knees and stuck her chin in one hand. She held the singing flute up to the firelight with the other. "I've been thinking about the song the flute played the other day."

As if the instrument understood Mae's words, it switched tunes. Mae let the melody run through her mind, then started to sing the words that formed on her lips.

> *Two hapennies, their carts in tow,*
> *Hi, hi, lo, lo*
> *Crossed a bridge and met a foe,*
> *Hi, hi, lo, lo*
> *The troll arose from deep below,*
> *Hi, hi, no, no*
> *With black eyes and fangs aglow,*
> *Hi, hi, no, no*
> *Will the hapennies' heads a' roll?*
> *Hi, hi, no, no*
> *The spell will turn the troll to coal,*
> *Hi, hi, yo, ho!*

Mae shrugged. "That's all I can remember." She sighed as the music faded. Firelight winked on the flute's warm wooden surface. She dropped the flute back in her pocket. "Why were the hapennies crossing the bridge in the song? Hapennies don't leave the Wedge."

"Hapennies don't leave the Wedge *anymore*," Callum said. "But there were some who were great traders before all the troll business. You've heard of them, I'm sure. The Great Expeditions, the hapennies used to call them. Fond of the word great, they are. Of course, I guess everything seems great when you are only the height of a miniature pony." Callum chuckled and then cleared his throat when Mae scowled.

"The travelers would journey great distances and return with wondrous goods. But the last trading expedition left before the troll invasion and never returned." Callum rose and walked to the bookshelves. "Perhaps I can find the other verses. I seem to remember a certain book..."

"My father was one of those that never returned from the last expedition. My mother writes in her letters that she is searching for him and that's why she's been gone so long."

Callum ran his finger over the leather spines. "Does she always write the same thing? That she is searching for your father?"

"Yes," Mae said. "And to do Gelbane's bidding and not cause trouble. The same be-good-until-I-get-back message in every letter."

"Don't you find that a bit odd?"

"Well, I do wish she'd tell me what she's seen and where she's been. What kind of adventures she's been having." Mae lifted her hand to stroke the blue orb necklace, forgetting that it had been lost. Momma had always kept the hope alive that her father would return, lighting a candle every night in the window—a beacon of light for him to find his way.

Aletta interrupted her thoughts. "Well, I have been thinking about your flute, too," she said. "About how it plays all by itself."

"You think it is enchanted, then?" Mae wound her arm around Aletta's, leaning against the warmth of her solid friend. She held her other hand out and made kissy noises at the weasel. When he ignored her, she plucked a few grapes off the stems and popped them in her mouth.

The weasel slowly appeared from under the chair and crept closer. Standing on his back legs, he sniffed at the table of snacks. Mae tossed him a grape and watched as he chased the fruit across the wooden floor. Catching the grape between his paws, the weasel smacked his lips as he ate it.

"Well, in a way I think your flute is enchanted, yes." Aletta lowered her voice. "It was something you said that night in the barn. You said playing your flute always soothed you when you were troubled with wishes."

The weasel padded back across the room for another snack. Mae scratched his head. His whiskers tickled her wrist. "What do wishes have to do with anything?"

"Every time you play, you infuse the flute with your dreams, hopes, and wishes. I think you are the one who has enchanted the flute, without even knowing it."

The weasel jumped into Mae's lap and curled up, shifting to show her his belly, like a cat. She petted his smooth fur. His ears were silky soft.

Callum turned from the shelves with a book in his hand. "I think you've surprised us both with how much magick you possess in that little body."

A funny feeling grew in Mae's belly. Her lap was warm from her new friend, but it wasn't that. She wasn't hungry, or perhaps she was, but it felt different from hunger. Possibility fluttered like butterfly wings. But it wasn't taking flight just yet. Mae pointed to the book in the wizard's hand. "Did you find the other verses?"

"What? Oh, no." Callum looked down at the opened book, scanning the page. "No, but I found something else that might help us..." The wizard lost himself in the words on the page.

Mae shrugged. The nursery song lingered in her thoughts. She hummed to herself.

Two Hapennies, their carts in tow
Hi, hi, lo, lo
They crossed a bridge and met a foe...

Bridge. She plucked another handful of grapes from the stem, popping one in her mouth.

Bridge...Gelbane...Mae crunched down on the firm fruit.

Gelbane hadn't followed Mae across the bridge when she fled the farm.

The remaining grapes in her hand fell to the floor.

"Gelbane is a troll," Mae whispered.

Chapter Eleven

"What did you say?" Callum asked. His brows furrowed over his hazel eyes. The book dropped from his hands.

"Gelbane is a troll!" Mae shouted, jumping up from her seat on the hearth. Her elbow caught the edge of the platter, and the food went flying.

The raven squawked and flapped his wings. The weasel batted a piece of sausage across the floor.

"Let's not jump to conclusions, Maewyn." Callum placed a settling hand on her shoulder, but Mae shook it off. Aletta's eyes were as big as mushrooms. Mae pointed at her. "You think so, too! It's the truth, Callum. Isn't it? That's what you were arguing about the other day."

Pacing between the hearth and the worktable, Mae uncurled her hand and pointed one finger each time she listed a reason. "Gelbane didn't follow me across the bridge. The scratches from her fingernails infected my leg. She doesn't like magick! The missing hapennies..." Mae's chest constricted as she grasped Callum's suspenders. "Trolls eat hapennies!"

Aletta crossed her arms. She stared at Callum, eyebrow raised in a near-perfect I-told-you-so arc. Her lips pursed.

Callum shook his head and swept off his hat, twisting it in his hands. "I refuse to believe that Gythal would make a mistake like that. There has to be another explanation." He shooed Mae away and paced in front of his worktable. "How would you explain the fact that Gelbane is in the Wedge in the first place?"

Mae shook her head. "I don't know, but I'm certain. When she is very angry with me...I see fangs. I always thought it was my imagination, but now I know it isn't."

Aletta shifted and clasped her hands in her lap. "What if Gelbane knew our Maewyn possessed the potential for magick? What if she doesn't like magick because it is the only thing that can reveal her true form?"

"But trolls don't have magick!" Mae exclaimed.

"Hapennies don't have magick, either," Aletta said.

Mae swallowed as a cold shiver ran through her. If hapennies could have magick, why couldn't trolls have magick, too?

"Gelbane could've conjured up a leyna charm to pass as a hapenny," Aletta said.

"What's a leyna charm?" Mae asked.

"It's a spell that produces a magickal skin that makes you look like something, or someone, else," Aletta answered.

"Trolls have been known to acquire a bit of magick." Callum nodded. "A few trolls in the past have been quite powerful. I suppose it is possible, but it is rare, and it still doesn't explain how she came to be in the Wedge in the first place."

How could a troll have gotten trapped in the Wedge? Maybe Gelbane was hiding and couldn't find a way out of the Wedge without being noticed. Maybe... "What if two trolls were responsible for the disappearances before?" Mae asked. "One was caught, and the other, Gelbane, hid. But then Gelbane was trapped in the Wedge by the spell on the bridge. Trolls couldn't get in, but they wouldn't be able to get out, either. She could have made the leyna to escape notice."

"Keeping up a constant disguise would take a great toll," Aletta said.

Mae snapped her fingers. "That's explains why she is always grouchy."

"Grouchy just goes with the territory." Callum turned to the bookshelf again. He ran his fingers over the ancient gold lettering on the spines until he reached the title he was looking for: *Trolls, Goblins, Hobgoblins, Brownies, Orcs, and other Nasty Faeries Who May or May Not Actually Exist—A Compendium.*

Mae sneezed as dust from the cover filled the room.

"I'll have to renew that housekeeping spell," Callum said. "It seems the feather dusters are getting a little lazy."

Callum laid the book on the worktable. Aletta joined him. He opened the cover and, using the braided end of his beard like a duster, swept it across the pages. "Trolls, if you would be so kind."

The pages of the book flipped rapidly, then stopped. Mae stood on tiptoe at the edge of the table. She could just see the illustration. Drawn in walnut-colored ink was a stout beast with long, disheveled hair and fangs sprouting out from under his upper lip. His arms were too long for his body and on the ends of his fingers were talons sharp as knives.

Callum read aloud.

"'According to Legend and hearsay, trolls can often be found near mountains, caves, and burrows, under hills, and in shaded dells. They are most often seen at dawn or dusk and at the edge of forests or wooded glades. Trolls stay out of the sun due to the drying nature of its rays on their skin, but like to wander on rainy days. They do not tolerate noise well, and it is said they can be driven away with the ringing of bells. Trolls are collectors of bits and baubles, the dirtier and more broken the better, although they do occasionally collect a shiny object for unknown reasons.'"

"That's why the dining table is so full of junk!" Mae exclaimed.

"'They are also known to steal property and women and enslave children,'" Callum continued. "'Trolls prefer to prey on small children and animals, but have been known to hunt full-grown men. Morose and sullen by nature, they are sometimes to blame for black magick. Though it is rare for a troll to possess magick, one that does can be extremely powerful. Troll magick may leave a magickal trace, seen as a glint of color, usually green. To trap a troll you must use the runes of protection... see page 345, index B.'"

As Callum finished reading, the pages flipped again. A loose piece of parchment sailed from the pages of the book. The raven whisked it out of the air and dropped it in front of Mae. She held it up to the light. The heading scrawled across the page read, "Gythal Saves the Wedge from Troll Invasion."

The animated drawing below the heading showed a tiny man in a flowing, black robe. If Mae hadn't known better, she would have thought he was a hapenny. As she gazed at the picture, it changed. The man raised a willowy wand above his head, and his sleeves scrunched up around his skinny elbows. His white beard was so long it folded upon itself on the ground before him.

A great number of large stones were piled up at the sides of the river in the picture. Mae could see the grimaces of the trolls as they turned into rock. She pointed to the circular lines and triangles carved into the granite pillars that anchored the bridge. "Are those the runes of protection?"

"Yes," Callum answered distractedly as he scanned the table of runes in the book.

Remy pecked at the clipping. "Maewyn," he cawed.

Mae shooed the raven away and studied the drawing. Aletta pointed to the strangely curved tree in the background. "There is the bowed elm that marks the edge of the Wedge. Of course, there is only one bridge in and out of the Wedge now. The others were destroyed during the Great Invasion."

"In this picture, the runes on the pillars look like they are twinkling," Mae said, pointing to the glittery shapes in the drawing.

"Yes, runes twinkle because of the magic they hold," Callum said. "It's more obvious in the light of the moon, but you can see it at other times, too, like during an eclipse, or at noon on the solstice days."

Mae ran her hands over the clipping, smoothing out the wrinkles. "But when I followed the raven here, to the cottage that first night, the runes weren't twinkling."

Callum snatched the clipping from the table. "No. No, it can't be."

Aletta braced her hands on the table. "What is it?"

Callum dropped his head in his hands. "I didn't want to believe it, but he tried to tell me. Before he passed...he tried to tell me."

Remy flew to Callum and perched on his shoulder. The wizard reached up and stroked the bird's chest.

Mae clenched and unclenched her fists. Her breath came short and quick. "The pillars have been disguised with leyna charms, too—that's why the runes don't twinkle in the moonlight when they should!"

The two wizards turned to Mae.

"First she took over my mother's house, and—" Mae swallowed. She didn't want to say the words that were forming in her mind. "With the runes gone, the hapennies are dinner."

"The runes can't just be erased away!" Callum cried. "They are protected by magick. I have checked them every week... How could something like this happen under my very nose? Someone is defacing the pillars, ruining the magick! A leyna charm... How could I have missed that?"

Aletta scowled at Callum. "Gelbane is opening the way for another troll invasion. How *could* you have missed that?"

Callum pointed to Aletta. "You cross that bridge more than I do! How did *you* miss it?"

Aletta's cheeks grew crimson. "I'm not the official Protector of the Wedge! You are!"

Mae scrambled to the top of the worktable and yelled at the top of her voice, "It doesn't matter! What matters is that we do something about it!" Her throat tightened and tears filled her eyes. "For Leif! For Reed! For Mother Underknoll! We've all been tricked!"

"If the trolls control the bridge," Callum's voice cracked, "the hapenny village is doomed."

"But how did she get across the bridge to destroy the protections?" Aletta murmured, choking back a sob.

"We'll need to discover her method before we make any moves," Callum said. His voice was somber. Gone were the laughing eyes and teasing tones.

Remy flapped his wings and cocked his head.

Aletta paced, chewing on a thumbnail.

Maewyn wrung the corner of her apron around her thumb. The table beneath her vibrated. "Do you feel that?"

Chapter Twelve

The teacups rattled against the saucers. In the distance, Mae heard a deep, steady rumble. She counted, "One...two... three..."

"Too long for a roll of thunder." Aletta crossed the room and pressed her nose to the windowpane, wand raised and ready.

The wizard's cottage trembled and groaned. The rumble faded, tumbling over the tops of the trees and into the night air.

Callum held up his braided wand. It trembled in his hand. "Move away from the window, Aletta."

Mae took her wand from her pocket and bent her knees, ready to spring.

A deafening creak, like trees bending in a gale, filled the wood.

The front door eased open, having been jarred from its latch.

An enormous, balled-up fist crashed onto the porch.

The tree-trunk fingers opened slowly.

Mae gasped as Reed, eyes closed and covered in mud, rolled out of the giant's hand and into the doorway.

"What have you done to him?" Aletta shrieked. The wizard ran to the boy.

"Reed!" Mae jumped from the table and followed Aletta, tugging her sleeve. "Look!" Mae pointed to Reed's chest, rising rhythmically. "He's breathing."

An enormous face, carved with wrinkles as deep as canyons, was framed by the open doorway. Eyes the size of wagon wheels peeked into the cottage. Gray, stringy hair, like weeds whose roots grow clinging to a rock face, spread out over his shoulders. He looked like a moving slice of the forest.

"A hapenny, the little ones, small peoples, was once kind to me," the giant's voice boomed across the room. "I would never, no, not once, hurt one of them."

Aletta scooped Reed up. He drooped like a sack of potatoes in her arms. "I'm going to clean him up a bit and get him into bed. I don't think he's injured, just exhausted and cold."

Mae stepped onto the porch. She craned her neck back to look in the giant's face. If he had found Reed, perhaps he'd seen Leif, too. "Where did you find him?"

"He was wandering in the forest, the trees, the wildwood. Must have lost his trail, departed from his path, forgot his way in the storm."

Mae wondered if all giants talked like this one. "Did you see another? His brother, Leif, he's missing, too...and Mother Underknoll."

The giant shook his head. "No, just that wee, little, pint-sized one. I knew he needed help, aid, assistance, and what better place to receive it than a wood wizard's cottage?"

"No better place." Callum stood behind Mae, his hand resting on the top of her head. "We want to thank you—er..."

"River Weed Starr," the giant said, sticking out his hand.

Callum grasped his finger and shook it.

"That's your name? River Weed Starr?" Mae asked.

"Yes." The giant nodded and rolled back on his heels. He draped a hand over his knee. "My mother named me after the first three things, objects, thingamajigs, she saw after giving birth, as is tradition, custom, legacy."

"So you were born by the river," Mae said, "in the summer when the weeds were tall."

"And on a clear night," Callum added.

Mae took hold of the corners of her apron and curtsied. "It is nice to meet you, River Weed Starr. My name is Maewyn Bridgepost. Thank you for rescuing my friend."

"Bridgepost, you say?" The giant's knees creaked as he shifted his weight. "That name has a familiar, friendly, nice feel on my tongue."

Callum cleared his throat. "Perhaps you knew her mother, Serena Bridgepost?"

River Weed Starr's eyes lit up. "Yes, I believe so." The giant turned his bare foot and pointed to the last toe. "Plucked a thorn, sticker, pricker, from my wee toe, she did. I have finally repaid, compensated, returned her kindness."

Maewyn threw her arms as far as she could around the giant's finger. "Thank you from the bottom of my tea cup. You have given me hope that Leif will be found as well."

Aletta stepped outside and placed her hand on Maewyn's shoulder. "Reed is asking for you."

Releasing River Weed Starr's finger, Mae ran into the cottage. She paused in the open doorway to her room and listened as Callum thanked the giant again for bringing him the hapenny boy. The wizard then lowered his voice and Mae swiveled her ears toward the front room to hear their whispers better.

"Have you seen anything strange happening in the area?"

The giant made a rumbling sound in his throat. "I thought you might want to know, comprehend, grasp. The trolls are up to something. There is far too much movement, migration, stirring, in the west for those lazy wretches not to be."

"Thank you, River Weed Starr. I appreciate the information."

The giant, peering over Callum's shoulder, caught Mae's eye and cleared his throat. "If ever you need my help, aid, assistance, just call my name. The forest, trees, wildwood, will find me."

Mae ducked into the room as Callum thanked River Weed Starr again. As the door latched, she turned her attention to Reed, who was propped up in the bed under the windows.

His face was pale. Even his freckles seemed faded. Sandy brown locks of hair cascaded over his brow. A washbasin sat at the foot of the bed, the water dingy from Aletta cleaning him up. He was dressed in one of Callum's shirts, but it was so big on him that the sleeves billowed over his hands.

"Reed, we thought we'd lost you." Mae dashed across the room and crawled up onto the bed to sit at her friend's side.

"Mae," Reed whispered. "I found you, but I was looking for someone else..." He reached for her hand and squeezed her fingers. "Gelbane..." His eyes blinked.

Mae tightened her hold on his hand. "You were looking for Gelbane?"

Reed shook his head and tried to talk again. "Leif..." His eyes shifted to the teacup on the table and then closed. "Gelbane...has..."

"What does Gelbane have?" Mae shook his shoulders. "Wake up, Reed. Tell me about Leif!"

Mae snatched the empty cup and peered into it. Bits of tea leaf were stuck to the sides. Her face shone back at her from the bottom. A familiar smell filled her nose and she knew there would be no talking to Reed until the morning. Aletta had dosed him with the sleeping tea. She banged the cup back onto its saucer. Next to it, on the top of the dresser, lay a small, carved turtle and a fishing fly. Mae picked up the fly. It was tied with red string and had downy black feathers. It looked just like the flies Callum was tying earlier. She dropped it in her pocket. Questions were taking form in her mind.

Reaching into the corner of the windowsill, Mae gathered the cobwebs clinging to the wooden casement. "Strands of spider's silky web, weave together for his bed."

Mae watched, amazed, as the cobweb grew upon itself, creating a hundred soft folds, and finally emerging as a soft, warm blanket. "It worked!" Her smile faded as she tucked the blanket under Reed's chin. He was safe, but what about Leif? What about Mother Underknoll?

Callum appeared in the doorway. "You've studied *Ahem's Book of Proper Grammar for Spell Casting.*"

"And she didn't even need her wand," Aletta added.

Mae nodded at the wizards. Her cheeks grew warm with embarrassment. "I couldn't sleep last night. Thought I'd do a little reading. Are you angry with me?"

"What?" Callum harrumphed. "What reason would I have for being angry?"

"I just thought...since I took the book without asking first...and tried a bit of magick..." Mae chewed the inside of her cheek.

Callum put his hands on her shoulders and kissed the top of her head. "No, Maewyn, I'm not angry. This is your home now. The books belong to you as much as anyone."

"And we all need to learn good spell writing." Aletta squeezed the top of Callum's arm with affection before gathering the washbasin from Reed's bed. She touched the magicked blanket and smiled. "I'd say this is a very useful spell." She nodded her approval as she left the room.

Mae pulled the fly from her pocket and held it up. "I found this next to Reed's teacup. Before he fell asleep he said he was looking for someone, but found me. Is it possible that he was looking for you, Callum?"

Callum nodded. "It was our little secret. We crossed paths one day at the bridge. He was upset that Leif had run off without him."

"And you leave these flies at their doorstep," Mae said. The threads were beginning to weave together.

Callum cocked his head to the side. "How did you know that?"

"Leif told me the fishing flies would just appear sometimes." Mae's lower lip trembled. She blinked the tears away. "He will be okay, right, Callum?"

"With a good friend like you, Reed is sure to get well soon."

Mae nodded, even though she had meant Leif. Would Leif be okay? She sopped her tears with the corner of her apron. She couldn't put her worries into words.

"Let him rest now. We'll question him in the morning and firm up our plans to find Leif." Callum guided her from the room and into the hallway. Mae peeked back at Reed as the wizard shut the door. He had wanted to tell her something about Gelbane and Leif before the sleeping tea took over, and she wasn't waiting for Reed to wake up to find out what it was.

Chapter Thirteen

The waxing gibbous moon shone through the window, lighting up the printed words of the article about Remington Gythal and the troll invasion. Mae crumpled it in her hand and tossed it across the room. How could she not have noticed there was a troll in her house for all these years? For that matter, how could a wizard not have noticed that the magick on the bridge was being destroyed? She sat up and threw her legs over the edge of the bed. She hadn't bothered to change into a nightgown or crawl under the soft sheets. She couldn't help but think of Leif as she gazed at his brother snoring softly across the room.

Mae slipped from the bed, reached for her boots, and shoved her feet into them. She patted her apron pocket, checking that her flute, raven, and wand were stowed safely as Callum's spell tightened the laces on her boots and tied little bows. Her ears swiveled to listen to the night noises in the cottage.

Callum's breathing was deep and even, and Aletta made little snorting noises. Even when she wasn't a pig, Aletta kind of sounded like one. Mae hoped the wizards were both sound sleepers. She reached into her hair and untangled Trina from her curls. The squirrel looked at her with sleepy eyes. "You have to stay here, Trina."

Trina shook her head, perked her whiskers, wiggled out of Mae's hand, and jumped into her apron pocket.

"No, Trina. You can't come." Mae pulled the little squirrel from her pocket and set her on the pillow. "You'll be safe from Gelbane here. Now stay put!"

Mae tiptoed across the room and scuttled up onto the foot of Reed's bed. He didn't stir as she stepped careful-like around him and pushed the window open.

The cloying fragrance of the night-blooming flowers hung in the still air, luring moths toward their nectar. Owls hooted. Coyotes yapped. Crickets chirped. The forest was alive with the sounds of night. Mae lifted her knee to the windowsill and pulled herself up. Shifting her body, she planted her feet in the flowerbox and slid the window shut. Mae pressed her nose against the glass and peered back into the room. She couldn't help but think of the last time she crawled out of a window.

Reed still slept, unmoving except for the rhythmic rise and fall of his chest. Trina stared from Mae's bed. Mae hoped the little squirrel wouldn't run to Callum and tattle.

Before she had a chance to change her mind, Mae jumped out of the flowerbox. She sprinted for the shortcut that would lead her to the Wedge.

Chapter Fourteen

"Shine brightly," Mae whispered, holding her wand in front of her. The end illuminated the pillars of the bridge. The runes were dark and magickless. She touched them and a jolt of energy sizzled up her arm as the *leyna* charm fizzled and fell away to reveal a vandalized stone face. Nervous moths rose in her stomach at what her wand revealed. Her hand shook as she touched the last pillar. The last bit of protection against the trolls.

A sharp crack, like a twig breaking underfoot, surprised Mae, and the light at the end of her wand winked out. Someone was approaching from the village. Mae scampered into the edge of the woods to hide. Remnants of cloud from the storm floated across the ivory moon, its half-light throwing more shadow than illumination. Mae peered into the blackness at the distant figure.

Lumpy and shambling, the figure drew near, carrying a large sack on its back. Something in the bag clinked together, metal on metal. Mae recognized the awkward gait. Gelbane!

Mae crouched, still as a fence post. She could hear Gelbane snuffle the air with her wide, flat nose, like she was savoring the aroma of a fatty stew.

"She's been here, that wretched spit of a girl," Gelbane muttered. "Snooping on me, no doubt."

A shiver ran through Mae. Gelbane had no idea how close she was to the truth. Whiskers had sprouted from Gelbane's chin and her ears were small and bald. They looked like withered, dried pears on the side of her head. Great yellow fangs protruded from under her top lip. Gelbane must have abandoned the *leyna* charm. That wasn't a good sign.

Gelbane dropped the lumpy sack on the road just before the bridge and untied its rope. The clouds blew away and the half moon shone again. She pulled out a pair of worn boots. The soles were thick and riddled with long iron spikes.

Of course! Maewyn slapped her hand against her forehead. Metal hurts magick…that's what Callum had said. Gelbane had found a way around Remington Gythal's protection spell.

Gelbane shoved her feet into the boots. A snigger floated on the air. "Those muffin-brained hapennies have no idea what's coming. Trusting some kitchen wizard to protect them. Well, they've got what's coming to them now. I can almost taste the hapenny stew." Drawing out a hammer and a chisel from the bag, Gelbane, in her true troll form, crossed the bridge. The nails scraped against the wooden planks. She settled the chisel against the last stone pillar and began to cut away the remaining trace of the runes protecting the Wedge.

Mae stood abruptly. She must get back to Callum and Aletta before Gelbane could tell the other trolls that the bridge was not protected anymore. A heavy hand closed over Mae's shoulder and another covered her mouth. She struggled as her captor pulled her off her feet and dragged her further into the trees. "Looky, Nord! Looky what we 'ave 'ere," a gruff whisper blew against Mae's ear. "A little spysie-wizey."

"What's going on over there?" Gelbane bellowed. "Nord? Taureck? Be that you?"

"'Tis me, Taureck!" The troll shouted back. "No worries, Gelbane, we jus' catched ourselves a little rabbit!"

"Well, be quiet, you lousy halfwits," Gelbane shouted back. "We don't want to give them any warnin's."

Mae cringed away from the sharp, metallic smell of the female troll's breath. She struggled in her grip as another troll emerged from the trees. He was large and broad across the shoulders. Greasy, dark hair hung around his jowls. He squeezed Mae's arm. "Should make a nice addition to our supper."

Mae aimed for his nose with her heel, but he grabbed her legs and cinched them in his grasp. Watery black eyes appraised her. "Nice an' pudgy, this 'un. Ain't like that string bean a coupla weeks ago."

They'd eaten Mother Underknoll! How had they captured her? Mae squirmed and tried to yell, but the claw against her mouth clamped down hard. She gagged at the feel of moist skin against her lips.

"Oh, Nord, we ain't ate a good hapenny stew in years, and we finally get some and ye still be complainin'," Taureck grumbled.

"Tie her up, Taureck. When Gelbane's chiseled the last of the runes from the pillar, we'll celebrate with this 'un!" Nord ambled off through the brush and bramble.

Mae struggled hard against her captor. Her mind was wild with fear. The few spells she knew whirled in her head. Mae concentrated on Taureck's arm and imagined red spots growing like a pox on the scrawny green wrist.

"What's that?" The troll's grip on Mae weakened. She shook her arm as if the spots would fall away. Mae wriggled loose, but was snatched by the collar.

"Oh, no, you don't. No hapenny tricksies are gonna work on me!"

A moan of anguish rumbled in Mae's throat. It was daft of her to think she could rid the Wedge of Gelbane and find Leif by herself. Sneaking out was the worst idea she'd ever had. Now she hoped Trina *would* tattle on her.

"Quit your caterwaulin'." Taureck bound Mae's wrists with a scratchy bit of rope. Mae tried to run again, but the troll shoved her to the ground with a long arm. Mae spat out leaves as her feet were tied together. The troll rolled Mae onto her back and chucked her under the chin with a bone-thin finger.

"You be so small, you be cookin' fast; you'll see. The other one was taller, but she only screamed for a few minutes. She was so easy to lure across the bridge. Pity she put that baby down first, though. I haven't had flesh that tender in a lifetime."

"That is a terrible thing to say." Mae scooched away from the troll's touch and cowered against a tree.

Taureck flashed a black-toothed grin and swiped at the stringy red hair falling across her face. Ripping a piece of thin material from her filthy vest, Taureck tried to stuff it into Mae's mouth. Mae turned her head and clenched her teeth. The troll grabbed her face, claws pushing into skin. "Terrible? You're gonna find out just how terrible I can be."

Reluctantly, Mae opened her mouth so the troll would release her grip. She couldn't fight back if she was scratched and infected again.

"That's a good hapenny. Always willin' to please, the lot of ye be." Taureck stuffed the dirty rag in. Mae bit down hard on the troll's finger.

"Owzies!" Taureck pulled her finger from Mae's mouth and shook it in the air. "You be the first one I eats!" A skeletal finger pulled a rattling bone necklace from under her faded blue corset. "And your teeth will make pretty baublies on my necklace."

Mae fought against the panic building in her mind as the troll pushed herself off Mae and ambled away with a rolling gait. Mae turned her wrists in the binding. She turned and twisted her arm. The rope burned her skin. She wished she hadn't made Trina stay at the cottage. Her sharp teeth would've made quick work of the ratty rope. Mae's mind spun as she tried to remember some kind of helpful spell. She fought against the tears building behind her eyes and the tightness in her throat. Crying wouldn't help anything.

Taureck had a smoky fire started when Nord strolled back through the trees. His yellowed fangs anchored a leering smile. "Gelbane said we can't eat that 'un yet. She wants us to bring her the little morsel."

One of Mae's hands slipped through the binding. She shook the rope loose from the other. She wasn't sticking around for Gelbane to see her.

"Bring it to her?" Taureck shrieked. "But I caughts it, and I'm hungry!"

"Don't matter. Gelbane said she's keeping it with the other 'un for the feasty tonight."

Mae shrieked against her gag. The other one? That's what Reed was trying to tell her. Gelbane had Leif! Mae sagged against the tree. She had no choice now. The easiest way to get to Leif was to let Gelbane take her. She wouldn't be able to cross the bridge without Gelbane seeing her. She forced her hand back into the binding.

Taureck screwed up her face. "'Gelbane said, Gelbane said'! Do you always do what Gelbane said?"

"You and me, we're to go to the others and tell them the way's made open." Nord grabbed a fallen limb from the ground. "Let's truss that 'un up so she don't try to kicksy us no more."

It was hard to breathe with the smelly rag in her mouth, and Mae's wrists stung from the rub of the rope. The runes were gone. The trolls controlled the bridge, which meant they were free to invade the village. She was too late to repair the runes, but at least she could help her friend and maybe warn the others.

Her flute and wand slid from her pocket and bounced into the grass as the two trolls trussed her to the branch. Mae shrieked and wiggled. She needed her wand! Taureck smacked her upside the head. "Be quiet, loathsome creature! Dinner's not supposed t' talk."

The trolls bent over with laughter as Mae swung like a suckling pig, stars filling her eyes. A smudge of daylight crept into the eastern sky. Her heart sank into her apron pocket as Taureck noticed the flute in the grass. The troll picked it up and stroked the shiny finish.

"Whatcha find, Taureck?" Nord asked.

Taureck folded the flute protectively in her hand. "Nuttin', just some shiny bits of wood."

"Let's go, then." Nord scowled. "Gelbane is waitin' on us, and you know she don't like to waitey."

Mae bounced painfully as the trolls lumbered along the wooded path.

Nord halted at the bridge, eyeing it with uncertainty. "Uh, ladies first."

Taureck shoved the pole Mae was trussed to into Nord, pushing him toward the planks of the bridge. "Oh, no. I insist you have the pleasure."

"But—I—"

"Let's go, you lowly good-for-nothings!" Gelbane shrieked. "We don't have time for your ninny-naggin'. The magick's gone!"

Nord stepped forward with hesitance, searching for the wood of the bridge with the tip of his toe. One eye was pinched shut; the other was only half open. Mae heard him take a deep, nervous breath. Mae held her breath, too. Perhaps luck was with her. Maybe Gelbane didn't quite finish the job.

Nord planted his foot on the bridge and froze.

A breeze sped through the trees.

The leaves rattled.

"C'mon, nitwit!" Gelbane advanced over the bridge and gave Nord's head a swipe with her fist. "You be alive. 'Tis a relief to know I did the job right."

Nord and Taureck exchanged a glance.

"Let me see what you've got there." Gelbane bent to peer at Mae. She ran a stubby finger across Mae's cheek as a wicked smile spread across her face. "Looks like you caught my runaway."

"She bit me, so she's the first 'un to go!" Taureck cackled.

"No, she's the last. I'm going to enjoy the look on her face when I eat her friends." Gelbane plucked the gag from Mae's mouth. "What do you have to say about that?"

Mae's stomach churned with loathing. She scowled at Gelbane but did not answer. The wicked snigger Mae had heard too often in the last six years settled over the fields.

"Follow me quickly." Gelbane turned down the path. "You need to be gone before the Wedge awakes."

Sooner than Mae could believe, they were halfway down the path that would take them to her home. In the dim light of dawn, the flowers growing out of the earthen roof were wilted and sad. The tree branches drooped to the ground. The rooster crowed at the rising sun. The chickens clucked sleepily from the trees at the edge of the forest. Mae hoped she wasn't hearing the rooster's crow for the last time.

Gelbane slammed the front door open and gestured to the hallway. "Put her in the cage with the other one."

Mae craned her neck to peer around the trolls and into Gelbane's workroom. Leif stared at her, his fingers clenched around the iron bars.

Leif! Leif *was* the creature she'd glimpsed in the cage!

The trolls dropped her on the floor and Taureck hissed, baring her fangs. Leif cowered into the corner while Gelbane opened the cage door. Nord cut Mae from the branch and shoved her into the cage.

"Don't be bruisin' our dinner, nitwit!" Gelbane growled.

Mae yanked the gag from her mouth and threw her arms around her friend.

Gelbane turned the key in the heavy lock and pointed to Taureck. "Go, fetch me some breakfast. And be quick about it."

Taureck pointed to Mae. "Why don't you make her do it?"

Gelbane bared her fangs. "I've got other plans for her."

In a tantrum, Taureck stormed out of the workshop.

"See you soon." Saliva dripped from Nord's fangs as he waggled his tongue in their direction and poked a claw through the bars, like a child poking at a rabbit in a cage.

"Or maybe I should say, taste you soon. My mouth is watering already." He sniffed the air. "Mmm...sweetmeats..."

Gelbane knocked him upside the head. "Over-anxious hapennies turn sour. Now leave 'em be and wipe that drool from your fangs." Gelbane sneered. "If anyone's mouth should be watering, it should be mine."

Taureck returned with three eggs clutched in her hand. "Should I put 'em in the pot for ya, too?" Taureck sneered.

Gelbane smashed the eggs in Taureck's hands. "How sick I am of eating eggs." Stringy yolk plopped onto the floor. "What I really want is the sweet taste of hapenny stew. Do you know how many years it's been since I last tasted the soft flesh of a hapenny?"

Taureck held up her sticky claws and tried to count them. "Um...three?"

Nord smiled and nodded his head in agreement.

"Six, you idiots!" Gelbane whirled on the two trolls, swinging her fist and thumping Nord on the head again. "Six long years it's taken me to chisel those runes away. Six long years I've pretended to be a nasty hapenny. Six. Disgustingly. Unsoiled. Years!"

Nord rubbed the lump on his head. "Why didn't you just eat 'er?"

"And have no one to do me chores?" Gelbane shrieked. "I wasn't gonna work like a hapenny, just 'cuz I looked like one!" Gelbane turned to Mae. "Your mother was nice and fatty. I suppose you'll taste just as sweet, even if you are just a bite."

"You ate my *mother*?" Mae screamed. "But—"

"But what, *dear one*?" A smirk slowly spread on Gelbane's face. "What about the letters she's written you promising to come home soon? Hapennies are so easy to fool."

"You wrote them," Mae said, "to keep me around." Tears burned in her eyes. Her heart sped. The clench of her fingers around the cage bars turned her knuckles white.

"That's right. My, you've become so smart. Too smart for your own good. But it doesn't matter. There's nothing you can do about it. My magick is stronger than yours." She turned to Nord and Taureck.

Mae glared at her former guardian's backside. She wished she could pull every one of Gelbane's teeth from her vile mouth. A red-hot hatred built in the pit of her stomach.

Gelbane pulled a copper pipe from her pocket and gave it to Nord. "Use my wand if you have to. She has a little bit of magick, but she don't know how to use it yet. Otherwise, I would've been discovered long ago. Just make sure she don't escape."

Nord turned the pipe over in his hands. "What do I do with it?"

"Just point and flick!" Gelbane screeched.

Nord pointed it at Gelbane.

"Not at me!" Gelbane shoved the wand out of her face. "I can't trust you two with nothing important. I'm gonna go tell the others the way is clear. You two nitwits will stay and keep watch over these two. Can you handle that?"

Nord and Taureck nodded.

With a leer, Gelbane pointed to Mae. "Tonight, we feast!"

Chapter Fifteen

Nord scuttled to a broken chair and forced his butt into it, cradling the wand like a baby.

Taureck tried to follow Gelbane, but halted when Gelbane scowled at her. "Could you send a signal when you arrive with the others?"

"A signal?"

Shrugging, Taureck looked down at her shuffling feet. "I don't know, a hoot or somethin'."

"Like an owl?" Gelbane sneered.

Taureck smiled and nodded. "Yea, you can hoot like an owl when you reach the bridge." She pursed her lips and made a strangled sound.

Gelbane slapped her upside the head. "That don't sound like an owl! It sounds like a drowning cat. I think you'll hear an army of trolls approach, don't you?"

Gelbane stomped out of the room with a last leering look at Mae. Taureck slammed the door, but it bounced in its casing and didn't catch. "Good riddance," she muttered. She pointed a claw at Leif. "I'll satisfy my hunger with you this afternoon."

Taureck leered at Mae. "When your friend is turning on the spitty, you can imagine me cooking you as well. That should make a nice and sour meal for ol' Gelbane." Taureck laughed and shambled down the hallway without a second glance back.

"Where ya goin'?" Nord shrieked. "We're s'possda' keep an eye on 'em!"

Taureck's grumble sounded down the hallway. "They're caged up! Where they gonna go?"

Nord wiggled himself out of the chair and followed Taureck. There was a lot of grumbling and banging.

Mae pulled the gag from Leif's mouth.

"What are you doing here?" Leif whispered.

"Saving you!" Mae whispered back.

"You aren't doing a very good job of it, are you?" Leif said. "Now we're both dinner!"

An image of her mother formed in Mae's mind. Had her mother been trussed up before she was eaten? Had Gelbane threatened harm to Mae to make her mother go obediently? Or did she go down fighting? Her chest constricted. A well of tears built up in her eyes. They fell on the red welts that bubbled up on her skin from being trussed to the tree limb. She picked at the frayed ends of rope on Leif's wrists.

Leif leaned his forehead against hers, and when the ropes fell away, he gathered her in his arms. "I'm so sorry about your mother."

Even though they were caged and held prisoner by a couple of nasty trolls, Mae felt safe. She cried for her mother. And for her father, and for Mabel and her missing mother. Surely Callum and Aletta had noticed she was gone by now. Why did they not come looking for her? Perhaps they had been captured, too.

Leif's stomach growled. "It's been a long time since I've eaten. Nothing since supper last night."

Mae pulled away, wiped her eyes, and ran a sleeve under her nose. "At least you haven't been eaten! The longer we stay, the better the chances of *that*, though."

"And just how do you think we're going to get out?" Leif asked.

"Magick." Mae leaned her forehead against the cage bars.

"Hapenny magick," Leif scoffed. "And my mother spins gold from caterpillar tents."

"Remember all those strange things that would happen around the farm? All those things I got punished for?"

Leif nodded.

"I'm a wizard, Leif, maybe the next Protector of the Wedge, and Gelbane knew it."

Leif scowled. "It's hard to believe."

Mae clenched the bars in her hands and closed her eyes.

"What are you doing?" Leif asked.

"Be quiet. I need to concentrate!" She looked at Leif. "Unless you'd like to stay for dinner?"

"I don't want to be a troll's dinner. Not like Mother Underknoll." Leif's ears drooped and his nose twitched. "I'm just glad Reed was dawdling, or Gelbane would've snagged him, too."

Mae put a comforting hand on Leif's shoulder. "Reed did follow you that day. He knew Gelbane had you. And then he tried to find Callum's house to get help and got lost in the woods during the storm."

"Who is Callum?"

"He's the Protector of the Wedge. He's the one who leaves fishing flies on your doorstep, and he's been teaching me to control my magick. Anyway, a giant found Reed in the forest and brought him to Callum's house."

"A giant?" Leif frowned. "Your story keeps getting crazier."

Mae nodded. "I know, but it's true. The giant that found Reed is the same giant that my mother helped a long time ago. Don't you remember the story?"

Leif shook his head.

"She was working in the vegetable patch when she heard a strange sound. She searched the forest that borders our property, and she found a giant crying. His big fingers couldn't grasp a tiny thistle stuck in his toe, and it was very painful each time he took a step. So, my mother pulled the sticker from the giant's toe, and he promised one day to return the favor."

Leif's eyes were as big as saucers. "Was he really...giant?"

Mae nodded. "Until I met River Weed Starr, I thought my momma had just made up that story to entertain us. Now I know that many things are possible—including a hapenny, and unfortunately, trolls having magick."

Mae heard a snuffling from the back bedroom.

Leif's eyes grew wide again. "Are they coming back?"

"I don't know." Mae's ears swiveled toward the bedrooms. She heard creaks and groans, then snoring. Mae let the breath she was holding whistle out. "I think they fell asleep." Mae ran her hands through her hair and took a deep breath. "Whether you believe me or not, at least now you know the truth about Gelbane. Will you help me warn the others?"

Leif scowled. "Of course, I will. What kind of hapenny do you think I am?"

"Good." Mae grasped the cage bars again. She remembered the little weasel romping around Callum's cottage. The bars twitched like tails. Soon the cage door was wiggling with a mass of weasels. They scattered up and over the contraptions crowding the room. Piles of parts slid to the floor with a crash as the weasels scrambled about.

"Garden snakes probably would've been a quieter choice," Leif said.

"What can I say? I'm new at this!"

Leif grabbed Mae's hand and pulled her down the hallway toward the front door. He reached for the knob.

"Wait!" Mae pulled on his hand. "You go. I must get that wand from Nord."

Leif shook his head, but Mae pushed him out the door. "Go! Go warn the others! And whatever happens," Mae said, "don't let a troll scratch you."

Footstomps came down the hallway. "You ain't goin' nowhere but the spitty, sweetmeat!" Nord filled the narrow hall, fangs bared and oozing. He clutched the wand in his fist.

Mae backed toward the door. "You don't scare me."

"I don't scare ya? You should be scared. In a few short hours, the Wedge will be a feasty for trolls!"

"Not true! I sent Leif to warn the others." Mae took another step backward.

"How are a buncha little people gonna save the Wedge?" Nord sneered. "With their rakeys an' sewin' needles?"

"They rid the Wedge of a troll before." Mae's mind whirled as she reached behind her. She dared not look to see how close she was to the door.

Outside the wind howled. The door creaked on its hinges.

"With the help of an old an' befuddled wizard. Where's yer Protector now? Not that Callum could save the Wedge with his kitchen-witchery, anyways. What's he gonna do? Make blueberry pancakies to soothe my gnawing hunger? Wash the stench from me clothes?"

Mae held her hands up, palms toward Nord, as if she could hold the troll back with nothing but her own little hands. "I'm the Wedge's Protector now."

Nord let out a harsh laugh. The wand shone with a strange green cast in the morning light. "Even without this thing...I bet I can turn ye into a meal before ye turn me into a no-good stoney sentinel."

The troll flicked his wrist toward the door. Leif shrieked as he toppled to the ground. Mae gawked at her friend. Leif hadn't gone to warn the others! He'd been turned into a shiny copper teakettle. The surface winked in the morning sun.

A thump on the pantry window startled Mae. A heart-shaped nose pressed against the pane. Aletta!

"I can't eat a teapotty," Nord screeched. "What good is this thing?" He flipped the wand into the heaping trash pile on the table.

Mae took another step back. "What will you tell Gelbane when she realizes that you lost her wand?"

"*Hurjota!*" Callum's voice roared into the room.

Nord cowered and covered his head.

"Stones don't need to eat," Callum said. He stood in the doorway, wand raised.

Nord raised his hands, claws spread open. He widened his small eyes. "I wasn't gonna eaty her, not really. Just wanted ta scare her a little."

"Don't listen to him, Callum! Gelbane has gone to tell the other trolls that they can cross the bridge!"

Nord's fangs flashed. "Put your wand away. What can a girly-man like you do against a troll like me?"

Callum's hand shook. He knit his brows and closed the distance between him and Nord.

"Your magick ain't gonna worky on me...kitchen witchy!" With that insult, Nord hurled himself at Callum and knocked his wand from his grasp. Wizard and troll brawled on the floor. Magick flew around the room, pinging off the hearthstones and sizzling into the walls.

"Go, Mae!" Callum puffed. "Get out of here!"

Mae scooped the kettle from the doorway as Aletta entered the house in her human form. The raven swept in behind her. In his grasp was Mae's wand! She reached up with one hand as it tumbled from the bird's claw and caught it, gripping it in her tiny fist.

Aletta pointed her wand at Nord. "*Tan-ima silex silticus!*"

A red streak of light shot from Aletta's wand, striking Nord in the shoulder. The troll jumped off of Callum as his arm hardened from flesh to stone, from elbow to fingertips. Nord roared and bared his fangs. He stumbled in Aletta's direction as Callum got back to his feet.

Mae tightened her grip on the kettle. Aletta's spell wasn't like anything she'd heard before, but Mae had the feeling she was the one that would have to finish it. Mae pointed her wand at the troll and spoke the words of the old nursery rhyme. "Troll to coal!"

Nord cocked his head in shock as a blue streak of magic arced from the tip of Mae's wand. The troll's legs turned to heavy rock, sticking him in place. The sound of stone grinding together filled the house as Nord turned to black rock. He let out a last howl, his face screwed up into a snarl as it hardened.

Mae wiped her brow. "Now that's what a troll should look like."

Tiny cracks spiderwebbed throughout the rock, accompanied by a loud pop and then a hiss. Then the statue of Nord crumbled, filling the house with dust and debris.

Aletta coughed and waved her hand in front of her face.

"Good work, Maewyn." Callum stumbled toward her, his breath coming in short bursts. "You have the makings of a very powerful wizard indeed, even if your spell casting needs a little work."

Mae brushed the dust from her pinafore and stepped into the rubble. "There's another troll in the back bedroom."

Aletta hurried down the hallway, then rushed back into the hearth room. "It escaped out one of the windows."

"We have to warn the villagers," Callum said.

"And protect the Wedge," Mae added. "More trolls are coming." Tucking the kettle under her arm, Mae ran to the bridge, the footsteps of Callum and Aletta echoing behind her.

Chapter Sixteen

Mae's muscles ached. Her lungs burned. Not even when she'd followed the raven through the woods that moonlit night had she pushed herself so hard. It felt like an eternity ago, but it wasn't. In just a few short days, she'd gone from being a mistreated orphan to the Protector of the Wedge. And she took the responsibility seriously. Her feet pounded against the dirt path, her arm gripping the kettle that was her best friend.

She skidded around a bend as Callum and Aletta called for her to stop, but she didn't. Storm clouds were rolling in. Gelbane had always been in a better mood on a rainy day. And the book, *Trolls, Goblins, Hobgoblins, Brownies, Orcs, and other Nasty Faeries Who May or May Not Actually Exist...A Compendium*, had said that trolls were seen more often at dawn, dusk, and cloudy days. The trolls were sure to move in sooner without the sun's bright rays. She had to protect the bridge immediately, and she didn't even know if she could do it.

Mae slowed to peer into the forest shadows that surrounded the bridge. Nothing seemed out of the ordinary, yet. Did she have time to try to turn Leif back into himself? She would need his help. A brief break in the approaching storm let a ray of sunshine touch the bridge. That was all the encouragement Mae needed. She dropped the kettle in the grass and knelt beside it. Her heart raced with anxiety. "Leif, if you can hear me," she panted, "listen up. I know you are having a hard time believing I'm a wizard. And I'm not really sure of it all myself. I haven't learned a spell for this kind of thing, so I'm just going try to change you back the way I changed the cage bars into weasels. But I need your help. You have to believe in me or it won't work."

Aletta approached from behind, holding her side and panting. "I'm not used to running on two legs."

Tears rocked on the edges of Mae's eyelids. "I'm not sure I can do this, Aletta. What if I mess up?"

Aletta put her warm hand on Mae's shoulder. "Are we talking about Leif or the bridge?"

Mae nodded. "Does it matter?"

"Use what is in your heart. No spell could be more powerful."

"Will you do it, Aletta?"

Aletta shook her head. "My memories of Leif and the Wedge aren't as strong as yours."

Mae gripped her wand in one hand and placed the other on the kettle's shiny surface. Closing her eyes, she dipped into her well of memories. She pictured Leif tossing his head to scatter the curls that always framed his face, and the dimple that showed up when he laughed. A warm tingle ran through her arm. She dove deeper into the memory well.

She thought of the way he shuffled his feet in the dirt when he was upset, and stuffed his hands in his pockets when he really wanted to hold her hand. She remembered the times they fished off the bridge, jumped from his papa's hayloft, and chased the piglets. She remembered all the pinky swears made by the light of a candle. Mae remembered his comforting arms around her when her momma left. His strong grip when he'd saved her from falling into the river. He'd been there. Every time. Whenever she needed him. And she needed him now.

"Come back to me," she whispered. A soft breeze lifted her curls from her face and made the edges of her apron flutter. She heard a gasp and opened her eyes.

Leif was curled in the grass with his face pinched tight, arms gripping his knees. He slowly unwound and let out a huge sigh. "I knew you could do it."

"Leif!" Mae threw her arms around him and they tumbled in the grass. "I'm so glad you're all right!" She buried her head in his shoulder. Then she scowled and punched him in the arm. "Why didn't you run? The trolls could've eaten you!"

"I deserved that." Leif rubbed his arm. "But I couldn't leave you behind. Wizard or not."

"You believe me?"

Leif shrugged. "I guess." His dimple pulled at his cheek when he smiled. Mae gave him another squeeze and then rolled to her knees.

Leif groaned as he stood. "My muscles are so stiff—you've no idea what it feels like to be stuffed into a copper kettle."

"Well, we're gonna know what it feels like to be stuffed into a troll's belly if we don't find a way to protect ourselves. We have to warn everyone."

Leif pointed across the river. "Trolls!" The shadows in the forest were lumpy and shifting in an unnatural fashion. "What if the villagers don't believe me?"

"They will," Aletta said. "You've been missing for days, right?"

Leif nodded.

"So, go to your father first. Tell him what happened," Mae said. "He'll help you convince the others to fight."

"And Callum should be in the village square by now. He'll back your word as well," Aletta added. "Go, Leif! We're running out of time."

Leif's eyes were wide with fright. Mae kissed his cheek. "Go! We'll be fine."

His eyes darted from Mae to Aletta and back. "I can't leave you."

"You must!" Mae cried.

"I'll be back as soon as I can. Protect her, Aletta, please." Leif turned and ran for the village.

Aletta scanned the edge of the forest. "I can't help you with the runes, Mae, but I can keep the trolls at bay for a while. Are you ready?"

Mae nodded. She took a deep breath and stepped onto the wooden planks of the bridge. The boards squeaked beneath her. She felt the beady stares of the trolls pierce her skin. Above her, the birds shrieked through the thick crown of the forest. Mae gripped her wand and scurried across the bridge.

Gelbane had left deep gouges in the stone face of each pillar. Even if Mae could repair the damage, would it be strong enough to hold back an army of trolls? Perhaps she should convince the village to get rid of the bridge. The number of shifting shadows in the forest grew as the sky darkened from the coming storm. Mae shook her head to clear her thoughts. This was no time for doubts.

The tip of her wand scratched against the surface as Mae traced the shapes of the runes onto the pillar, over and over, but the runes would not carve into the face. She'd memorized the protection symbols from the newspaper clipping. She was clearly picturing them in her head. Why wasn't it working?

Beads of sweat popped to the surface of her forehead. She swiped at the dampening curls that stuck to her face.

Clouds piled on top of each other. Thunder grumbled in the distance. A troll stepped out of the trees and onto the path. Aletta shifted from foot to foot. She gripped her wand. "How much longer, Mae?"

"It's not working!" she whispered. "What am I supposed to do?"

"*Tan-ima silex silticus!*" Aletta's voice rang in Mae's ear. The troll stopped as the spell narrowly missed him, ricocheting off the path and striking a tree. A loud cracking reverberated through the forest as the tree's trunk turned to stone. Like a fire that has been put out suddenly with a pail of water, the leaves hissed as they were silenced.

"Use your heart, Mae. The magick has to come from you." Aletta raised her wand again and yelled across the path. "I won't miss next time!"

Mae crouched, leaning her forehead against the pillar. The thunder grew closer. How did Callum and Aletta ever think a lone hapenny would be strong enough to be the Protector of the Wedge? She might have a bit of magick, but it wasn't strong enough. She sniffed back tears. Crying wouldn't help anything, either, but she couldn't do this on her own.

"Don't give up now, Maewyn!" Aletta hissed as she let another spell fly. This one landed on its mark, and a stone troll grew up in the middle of the path. Rain began to fall, stinging against Mae's cheeks. Another troll stepped bravely onto the path.

Behind her, Mae heard footfalls. She glanced over her shoulder.

Leif and Callum rushed around the bend, leading a band of hapennies.

Chapter Seventeen

Mr. Whiteknoll was at the front of the line, his lavender cape swirling about his ankles, small bells sewn to the hem. He gripped an upholstery needle in one hand and a pair of scissors in the other. Ms. Gnarlroot carried a shovel, while Farmer Burrbridge carried a pitchfork. Even old Widow Bridgepath had shown up, her knuckles white from the grip of her wrinkled hands around the handle of a cast-iron pan. Many others were there, too, with whatever they could grab that might keep a troll at bay. More hapennies trickled in behind them. Some wore pots on their heads like helmets. Others had real armor, remnants of a time when the Wedge didn't have a wizard to help safeguard their village. The villagers had come to protect the Wedge. They had come to protect her.

Mae took a deep breath. "I'm the smallest hapenny in the village. I don't know if I can do this."

"It isn't the size of your body that matters," Callum said, "but the size of your heart."

Leif walked to her and folded her hand in his. "I'll stand right beside you, no matter what."

A large raven settled at the top of a bridge pillar. "Come, Maewyn!" he called.

Today, Remy's calling of her name felt like a battle cry. Maybe it didn't matter what size you were, as long as you were in it with friends, with *family*. She pictured the villagers' homes nestled in the tree roots and dug into the hillsides, their loved ones counting on them for protection. Her heart swelled at the sight of the wrinkled face of Widow Bridgepath and of Leif's dad, Mr. Burrbridge, weapons quaking with anticipation.

"It's high time a hapenny was born a Protector!" Mr. Whiteknoll yelled.

"Hear, hear!" Mr. Burrbridge cheered.

With renewed determination, Mae stowed the wand in her pocket and fished out the raven carving Leif had made for her. She tightened her grasp on Leif's hand and closed her other fist around the wooden carving. She pictured a great raven in her mind. His color was as deep as a moonless night, his talons as sharp as knives. The raven's eyes were keen, able to see for miles. She felt a great wind stir as the bird beat its wings. Intense magick stirred within her, power coming from deep within.

Mae filled the bird in her mind with the memories of her mother and father and the songs and stories of the hapenny people. She filled the raven with hope and love until pinpricks of light shone through his feathers like stars in the sky. Mae let the magick flow through her and into the carving gripped in her hand. Her legs shook uncontrollably; her arms felt like heavy bags of flour, and still she poured her memories into the raven, until her legs buckled underneath her. The crowd of hapennies gasped as she collapsed against the rough surface of the pillar.

Chapter Eighteen

Someone was shaking her and calling her name. Mae blinked and looked into Leif's face.

"Are you all right?" Aletta was close, too.

She turned to see lines of worry etched across the wizard's forehead.

The hapenny villagers had drawn close, stomping their feet in rhythm and chanting, all ears perked forward and alert, noses twitching, weapons poised for action. Mae uncurled her fingers. Sawdust blew from her palm. The carving Leif had given her was destroyed.

"Oh, I'm so sorry, Leif. Your beautiful carving."

"Forget about it; it isn't important," Leif said. "It can be replaced."

"What's happening?" Mae asked.

Aletta pulled Mae to her feet. "Leif, take her to Callum, she needs to rest. You've done what you could, Mae. Now it's up to the rest of us."

Mae peered around Aletta. Where the pillars of the bridge used to be, four great stone ravens stood sentinel. They looked identical: wings tucked tight to their bodies, feathers that stuck out haphazardly on their chests, long, curving beaks. Each bird was facing a different direction—north, south, east, and west. On each of their chests, a medallion nestled into their feathers bearing the runes of protection. The black stone they were made of shone like a new iron skillet through the rain. Mae was awed by the ravens' size and gleaming black eyes. Would her magick be strong enough to protect the Wedge from the horde of trolls?

Mae picked Gelbane out of the crowd on the other side of the bridge. Gelbane pointed at her and licked her lips. Thunder clapped. The lightning that followed made the trolls' faces look even more sunken and starved. The sound of the village bell tolled in the distance.

Aletta spun from Mae and a spout of magick erupted from her wand. Still the trolls kept coming. The army of hapennies pushed forward, swallowing Mae and Leif in their numbers. Callum tugged her from the crush. "Come, Maewyn. You need to rest."

Mae yanked her arm from the wizard's grasp. "No! I will not leave my friends. We have to help fight!"

Callum's shoulders sank. "I'm a kitchen witch, Mae. I'm not a great warrior."

"And I'm the smallest hapenny in the Wedge, but I'm not going to stand by as my friends become troll chow." Mae pushed through the crowd, leaving Callum and Leif behind. The wind drove the rain into her already sodden clothes. Her body ached with weariness and cold, but she stood shoulder to hip with Aletta and raised her wand.

There were more stone trolls than Mae could count on her fingers and toes. She peered into the mass of green and aimed for the wide-hipped Gelbane. "Troll to coal!" A blue zap of magick erupted from the tip of her wand and struck its mark. Gelbane's legs turned to stone, and she was stuck in the middle of the path. Another troll quickly took cover behind her. Gelbane pivoted and hit the troll with her meaty fists. "You'll not cower behind me! I could've kept all the hapennies to myself and instead I decided to share the lot with you ungrateful, no-good nitwits!"

The troll darted away from Gelbane's flashing fists and stinging words. It was Taureck! She quickly seized another to hide behind, but her cover was soon hit by a stone spell cast by Aletta. His arm crumbled from his body.

"I can't hold them anymore, Mae," Aletta said. "There are too many, and my magick is fading." She pulled on Mae's sleeve, dragging her off the bridge.

"What are we to do, then?" Mae asked.

"We fight! Like warriors! Grab whatever you can find!"

A mass of trolls gathered at the edge of the river. They moved warily closer. Taureck pushed a smaller troll onto the middle of the bridge. The troll stumbled and froze, a grimace on his face and his fists curled tight. When nothing happened, he relaxed and sneered at the villagers. His shoulders straightened with confidence. He bared his claws and hissed at the hapennies.

Lightening rippled across the surface of one stone raven, and then a second. "Get off the bridge!" Mae yelled to the villagers, waving frantically for them to retreat.

"Yes! You'd better run and hide, my little sweetmeats," Taureck cackled. "Cos' we're coming over for dinner!"

The trolls rushed across the bridge. The hapennies fell back. The clang of metal against metal rang in the air. The earth shook beneath her as the trolls grappled with her friends and neighbors. Mae's magick hadn't been enough.

The storm picked up, the wind howling through the trees and throwing the rain like tiny darts. The forest canopy flashed its silver underside. Mae scanned the field for Leif. He was poking a troll with the tines of a pitchfork while his father beat the troll with a shovel. Mr. Whiteknoll snapped the scissors at another attacker's grasping claws. Blood dotted the tailor's sleeve.

A great flash of lightning turned the sky a brilliant, hot white. Black stone turned to ebony feathers and gripping claws as the ravens unfurled their wings and took to the air. A piercing cry echoed over the field. Mae winced and covered her ears. The trolls cowered at the deafening sound. Thunder rumbled, adding to the cacophony. Sharp beaks snatched and grabbed, throwing trolls into the rushing river. Others were deposited, screaming, into the treetops.

Everywhere, hapennies clashed with trolls, but slowly Mae saw the rush of battle turning to their advantage. Suddenly, from over the hill, a strange army approached, with Callum in the lead. The wizard pointed his wand at the melee, and every broom and mop in the village entered the battle, followed by the swarm of weasels from the farm and a gang of kitchen knives darting around like murderous dragonflies. The weasels chased the trolls and nipped at their heels, while the knives poked and prodded the trolls over the bridge. Callum smiled as the broom soldiers swept the field clean.

The hapennies cheered at the backs of the fleeing invaders. The ravens settled on the four corners of the bridge and smoothed their feathers. One by one, they lifted their heads, filling the sky with their piercing call. The lightning that rippled over them before they came to life flowed over their feathers again. The sound of retreating thunder echoed over the Wedge as the raven guardians returned to their stone state. The stinging rain slowed to a drizzle. Mae felt someone reach for her hand and knew it was Leif. She interlaced her fingers with his.

"You did it, Mae," he whispered in her ear.

"We did it together," Mae said. "If it wasn't for your raven, I don't know if I could have done it."

Mr. Whiteknoll stumbled toward them, holding out his arm. His sleeve was torn and saturated with blood. He wobbled and fell to his knees. Mae scanned the crowd of warriors. Many hapennies were injured. Too many, but at least no more would become dinner. Widow Bridgepath was busy cleaning scrapes and binding bruises. Callum was tending to the more serious cases. Mae pointed to the line of trees where villagers were carrying those who had been injured. "Leif, can you take Mr. Whiteknoll to Callum? I need to find Aletta."

Leif draped Mr. Whiteknoll's uninjured arm around his shoulders and pulled him to his feet. "Be careful, Mae."

Mae nodded. "I will." She lifted her voice above the celebrations and the drizzling rain. "Do not celebrate yet!"

The hapennies quieted. Hundreds of faces streaked with mud and weariness turned to her. Mr. Gnarlroot stepped from the crowd. "But the trolls have fled. And your spell, it was brilliant. We've won the day, Maewyn."

"I know it feels like that, but..." Mae shook her head. A funny feeling was stirring in her belly. "Did anyone see a skinny troll with stringy red hair? She was wearing a faded blue corset and a necklace made of bones."

The crowd shook their heads and talked amongst themselves.

"Not since the trolls rushed over the bridge," Mr. Burrbridge answered.

The last time Mae had seen Taureck, Aletta had just pulled Mae back and told her to fight like a warrior. That was the last time she'd seen Aletta as well. Sweat broke out on Mae's forehead. She strode over the bridge, her footfalls tapping against the wooden slats. The villagers replaced their helmets and gathered their weapons.

Her heart raced as she approached Gelbane, feet still planted in the middle of the path. She raised her wand at her guardian, careful to stay out of her claws' reach. "My mother always said folks should be given a second chance."

Gelbane's eyes brightened. "You'll change me foot back to flesh?"

Mae raised her eyebrows. She should want to see Gelbane suffer, but she couldn't bring herself to do it, even if she had eaten her mother. "I'll change you, if you tell me where Taureck snuck off to."

The trees at the edge of the forest shook their leaves; cold droplets of water fell around Mae, bouncing into mud-filled puddles.

"You looking for me, sweetmeats?"

Mae jumped. Taureck slunk out of the forest, and Mae stepped away from both of the trolls.

"That doesn't count!" Gelbane shouted. "She came out afore I could tell on her!"

"Shut yer gob, Gelbane. She ain't gonna be fixin' your foots noways. She ain't got no magicks left. Just a little magicky for a little hapenny. That's all she gots." Taureck licked her scaly lips. "You shoulda let me eaty her this mornin'."

The ground rumbled under them, making Taureck flail her arms out to keep her balance. Mae bent her knees and held her place. "You want to test me, Taureck? I may be small and battle weary, but I think I've got at least one good spell left in me."

Mae shifted her glance over Taureck's shoulder. The trees were bending unnaturally.

"Who ya lookin' fer?" Taureck sneered. "Ain't no help comin'. Your little piggy friend took off through the woods before the battle was even over."

"If I were you, I would take off, too." Mae pointed to the trees.

Gelbane's eyes grew as wide as meatballs.

Taureck shuffled closer. "Oh, no, I ain't fallin' for your tricksies again."

Mae shrugged her shoulders. "Suit yourself."

An enormous hand swung through the air, scooping up Taureck by the seat of her knickers. She dangled high above Mae, pinched between two of River Weed Starr's fingers.

"You having a problem, issue, concern with this one, Mae?" The giant's voice carried over the Wedge.

Mae crossed her arms. "I was trying to convince Taureck that the Wedge is no place for the likes of her. But you know how stubborn trolls can be."

A slow smile spread across River Weed Starr's face.

Mae held up a finger. "Um, before you toss her, I'd really love to get my flute back. It belonged to my mother and Taureck stole it from me."

River Weed Star shook Taureck and she squealed. Mae's flute tumbled from her corset and fell into the grass. Mae scooped it up and held it close to her chest. The giant flicked his wrist, and the villagers *hurrahed* as Taureck went cartwheeling through the clouds.

Crouching, River Weed Starr knit his brows. He gestured to Gelbane. "You need help, aid, assistance with that one, too?"

"I have a plan for that one." Mae kissed the tip of the giant's nose. "Thank you, River Weed Starr."

The giant blushed. "Aw, corn shucks, any time, minute, moment you need me, Maewyn Bridgepost."

River Weed Starr bowed his head to the villagers who were gathered at the edge of the bridge, necks craned back, mouths hanging open like those of baby birds. Mae waved as the giant disappeared back into the forest. Rays of sunshine filtered through the thinning clouds. Steam rolled off the wet grass. She dropped her flute in her pocket and turned on Gelbane, wand raised.

"Please, please don't turn me into stone," Gelbane pleaded. "Think of all the years I took care of ye. Who would've taken you in if it wasn't for me?"

The tip of Mae's wand wavered. The crowd murmured and shuffled.

Mr. Whiteknoll stepped forward. "I would have taken her in."

"I would have cared for her, as well," Widow Bridgepath pushed forward.

A chorus of "me, too" resonated off the bridge.

Mae cleared the lump in her throat. "I wouldn't have needed anyone to take care of me if you hadn't have eaten my mother. *Verdantre!*"

Misty green leaves flowed from the tip of Mae's wand. She circled the troll as Gelbane's arms lengthened and her meaty fingers grew into spindly branches. Her skin darkened and split, thickening into bark. Gelbane howled as her toes spread root-like into the soil. "You said you would change me back! You miserable little twit! Curse you and your hapenny magick!"

Mae smiled as Gelbane's cries were swallowed by the growth of her new branches. "I said I would change you. I didn't say what I would change you into. I hope you find more happiness as a tree than you did as a troll."

Leaves unfurled and reached for the sky. Bright rays broke through the clouds and struck something caught in a lower limb of the Gelbane tree. It was her orb pendant! Mae slid her wand into her pocket and reached up to pluck the orb from the branch. She polished the surface on her apron, cracking it open at the hidden latch. A dark curl tied with a blue ribbon was nestled inside, the lock of her father's hair. Maewyn stroked the soft curl. Her throat tightened. Now she had both of her most prized possessions back. She snapped the orb back together, dropping it into her pocket.

Cheers echoed over the field. From the corner of her eye, Mae saw movement at the edge of the forest. Hooves beat against the muddy path. Mae raised her wand and braced herself for another fight. Around the bend came Reed, trotting toward her on the back of a pig.

"Aletta!" Mae squealed and ran to her friends.

"Reed!" Leif and his father yelled as they ran across the bridge. Reed dropped from Aletta's back and ran into their embrace.

"We thought we'd lost you," Mr. Burrbridge cried.

Words rushed out of Reed. "I saw Gelbane snatch Leif, Papa. So I followed her. She went to the river and yelled across and two trolls came out of the woods. She bared her fangs at them and I knew she was a troll, papa. I just knew. So I ran into the forest to find the Protector of the Wedge, but I didn't know where to look. And then the storm came and I was so cold, and I don't remember anything after that until I woke up in the wizard's cottage this morning."

"It's all right, son. You did well." Mr. Burrbridge tousled Reed's hair. Out popped a furry little face with bright eyes. Trina's tail flipped as she jumped from Reed's mass of curls to Mae's shoulder. Trina rubbed her head on Mae's cheek.

Mae stroked the squirrel's bushy tail. "I'm glad to see you, too, Trina."

Aletta put her arm around Mae and gave her a squeeze. "I went to get the ointment for Callum. I knew he would need it after the battle to treat those who had been scratched by the trolls. Do you want to come see if he needs any help?"

Mae nodded and let Aletta lead her away. Some of the villagers patted her back as she passed through. Others chanted her name. The seeds of dandelions floated into the air like confetti. Trina sat straight and tall on her shoulder, one hand gripping a lock of hair, the other waving to the crowd. On top of the rise, more hapennies gathered with their children in tow.

Leif's momma searched the crowd. Her eyes lit up as her gaze landed on Mr. Burrbridge, with Reed on his shoulder and Leif by his side. She gathered her skirts and raced down the hill.

"What's going to happen now, Aletta?" Mae asked.

"What do you mean?"

Mae stopped and fiddled with the corners of her apron. "Who will take care of the farm?"

"Well, I suppose Leif's dad could take the pigs, and we could find someone to adopt the chickens." Aletta gathered Mae's petite hands in hers. "You are the rightful Protector of the Wedge, Maewyn. There is still much you need to learn."

"Come, Maewyn!" Remy settled on a tree branch above Callum. He cocked his head, black eyes glinting in the sun. The raven glided down into the grass as Mae jogged to the tree.

Kneeling, she cupped her hand and smoothed the unruly feathers on the bird's head.

Mist grew and hovered around the bird. Mae backed away in surprise as feathers molted away, littering the grass. The mist thickened, forming the shape of a tiny man. He was barely two heads taller than Mae. His beard was so long it folded upon itself on the ground before him.

"Take care of all those hobgoblins running free in the forest," Remington Gythal said. "You have a responsibility to care for them now that you've brought them to life."

"Hobgoblins?" Callum raised an eyebrow.

Mae blushed. "I will."

"I know you will," the Great Protector said. "I'm so sorry, Maewyn, for the loss of your mother. Had I been a stronger wizard..."

"No, please, Remy," Mae interrupted. She swallowed to ease the tightness in her throat and wondered if the mention of her mother would always feel like this. "Your spells kept the

Wedge safe for these many years. My mother was grateful for that. We all are."

Remington Gythal surveyed the gathered villagers. "Fear no more, dear hapennies. The trolls are gone, and the Wedge is in good hands." The wind whistled across the field, pulling the wizard's ghostly image with it.

The crowd gasped and murmured, confused. Mae turned to the crowd. "When the Great Protector, Remington Gythal, put the protective charms on the bridge, he didn't know there was a troll still in the Wedge. She's been trapped here for six years."

"Gelbane!" Widow Bridgepath stabbed the earth with her shovel. "I always had a bad feeling about that woman." She shook her head. "I tried to warn your mother, but her heart held too much compassion for her own good."

"That's right," Mae said. "Gelbane was a troll. And she hid herself among us with a magickal skin, a *leyna* charm, which made her appear to be just another hapenny. She hid the damage she was causing to the pillars with a *leyna* charm, too. That's why we didn't know until it was almost too late."

"And that was the ghost of Gythal?" Leif stepped to the front of the crowd.

Aletta shook her head. "Not a ghost, more like a spirit or an energy."

Callum stepped up behind Mae and rested his hands on her shoulders. "He wasn't a wizard anymore. He used the last of his magick to change his spirit into the form of a raven in his one hundred twentieth year." Callum held up a hand to quiet the crowd. "If it is all right with the villagers of the Wedge, in the absence of her mother and father, Aletta and I would like to become Maewyn's guardians."

The crowd murmured excitedly. Mr. Burrbridge pushed his way forward. "Wizards don't live in the Wedge."

Widow Bridgepath pushed her way to the front of the crowd. "As the eldest hapenny, I can attest to the fact that it is not customary for humans, especially wizards, to live amongst us."

Mae's shoulders drooped. She hid her face behind Callum's trousers. She didn't want the villagers to see the tears forming in her eyes. To save her home only to be forced to leave it. It didn't seem fair.

"But," Widow Bridgepath continued, "under the circumstances, I believe we should allow it. Do the other town elders agree?"

Mae held her breath. Callum's warm hand squeezed her shoulder.

Widow Bridgepath cleared her throat. "Callum, Aletta, you are welcome to stay in the Wedge until Mae is grown and has truly learned in the art of magick. It would be best for all concerned."

Hearty voices full of joy filled the meadow. Mae nodded to Widow Bridgepath and smiled at the celebrating hapennies, until she saw Mr. Underknoll. His gaze was distant as he gently stroked the hand of the sleeping newlyborn in his arms. Ms. Gnarlroot accompanied him as he approached the wizards.

Ms. Gnarlroot's smile wavered. "I fear we've lost Mabel's mother to the trolls."

"Your fears are correct, Ms. Gnarlroot." Aletta placed a comforting hand on Mr. Underknoll's arm.

"I'm sorry for that and for you, Mae," Mr. Underknoll said. "I loved my wife more than any other hapenny in the Wedge, except this little one." He swayed from foot to foot, rocking

Mabel. His lower lip trembled and he tried to hold back tears, but they slipped down his cheeks like water from a spigot.

"The whole village talked about how terrible Gelbane was," Ms. Gnarlroot said. "I don't know why no one stepped in to help you. I suppose we were all scared of her, but you, you faced your fear and you saved our village. We are all greatly indebted to you, Maewyn."

"I had a lot of help." Mae smoothed an unruly curl sticking up from the baby's tangle of red hair. "Can I ask a favor of you? I know you'll take good care of her, Mr. Underknoll, but…" Mae stroked the pudgy little fingers sticking out from the soft pink dress sleeves. "Sing to her, and never forget to tell her how much her mother loved her."

"I will, Maewyn, don't you worry." Mr. Underknoll swiped another tear from his cheek.

"And one more thing?" Mae added. "If strange things start happening at your house, don't blame it on Mabel, but the magick that is within her."

Mr. Underknoll and Ms. Gnarlroot nodded and disappeared into the crowd.

Mae's stomach rumbled. She put her hand across her belly to quiet the complaining.

"I think you've missed breakfast again." Callum laughed and grabbed Mae's hand. He winked at Aletta. "Wands at the ready?"

The wizards lifted their wands. With a wave things appeared: decorated tables piled high with bread, cheese, and all manner of fruits and vegetables. Platters of steaming meat appeared, followed by pitchers full of dark purple wedgeberry rum. Colorful banners snapped in the breeze. Flowers bloomed in the field. Callum grabbed a glass from the table and filled it with wedgeberry rum. The crowd quieted. "For Serena Bridgepost and Mother Underknoll. May their memories never fade. And for our little wizard, the first hapenny to reclaim the ancient magick within all of you."

The crowd roared its approval.

"I'll drink to that," Aletta said. She filled a glass, and the two wizards clinked rims before downing the sweet wine.

Over the bridge shuffled the hobgoblins Mae had brought to life in the woods. Their polka dotted hats bobbed and weaved. They carried musical instruments, which they strummed or blew or banged as they approached. Lively music filled hill and dale.

Leif grabbed Mae's hand, pulling her into a circle of dancing hapennies. "I didn't get the chance to thank you properly, Mae."

Mae took two steps to the right and twirled under Leif's arm. "Properly? For what?"

"For saving my life." Leif hopped to the left, pulling Mae with him. "Twice."

"You would've done the same for me. Best friends do that kind of thing for each other."

Mae stumbled and Leif pulled her close. "I love you, Mae. You're my best friend...maybe even more."

Mae blushed.

"If you are going to be the next Protector's best friend, and maybe even more," Callum said, interrupting their dance, "you'll need to learn some magick."

"But—but I don't have any magick," Leif said.

"That's not true," Mae said. "It was your raven carving that made my magick strong enough to protect the village."

Leif gave Mae a worried look as Callum put his arm around him, leading Leif away from the dancing crowd. "A totem maker. Now that is some powerful magick, indeed."

Author's Note

Sometimes stories don't behave the way you expect them too. *Hapenny Magick* is a clear example of a story misbehaving. What began as a picture book about the circle of life, titled *The White Raven*, demanded to be more. From this 700-word manuscript grew a story about a community pulling together.

My friend, and fellow fairy artist, Linda Ravenscroft (www. lindaravenscroft.com), drew some sketches based on my faerie dolls to illustrate *The White Raven*, and I have included them with her permission. I hope you enjoy reading the short story that inspired *Hapenny Magick*, a tale about how even the smallest voice can create change.

The White Raven
by Jennifer Carson

One dark night in a long-ago time, there was a small boy named Kieran. By moonlight he stumbled through the woods, following a white raven. After many hours the bird settled on the smoking chimney of a cottage nestled deep in the forest.

When Kieran poked his head in through the open door, a sweet odor tickled his nose. His belly grumbled as he watched a wizard stir something in a pot hanging over the fire. Kieran wiped his nose with a tattered sleeve. "Please, sir, a crust of bread?"

The wizard turned from the hearth and smiled at the boy. "I can do better than that," he said. The wizard approached and pulled a white feather from the boy's tangled hair. Twirling it between his fingers, the wizard led Kieran to a small meadow just beyond the cottage. He plucked kernels from a few stalks of wheat and tucked them in Kieran's hand, followed by a splash of water from the creek.

"My name is Gannon," the wizard said. He tugged on the braided tail of his beard and held it aloft, like a wand. "And

now, my young friend, now is the right time for a spell. A sweetened loaf is the prize. Grains of flour quickly rise!" A steaming loaf of bread appeared in Kieran's hand. "Would you like to learn magic?"

With his mouth full, Kieran nodded, his eyes wide with excitement.

"Very well, we'll start your lessons as soon as you are dressed!"

"But I am dressed," Kieran protested.

Gannon's sapphire eyes twinkled with amusement. "You aren't dressed properly for a wizard's apprentice."

Kieran wrapped his arms around himself as he followed Gannon back into the cottage. "Then what shall I wear?"

The wizard bent to his worktable, found some snippets of yarn, and stuffed them into his fist. "Say, 'Mend and patch, cut and sew; new clothes I need, from head to toe!'"

Kieran repeated the spell and Gannon threw the snippets of yarn into the air. The yarn transformed into a pointed hat and a wizard's robe. Kieran pulled the hat on and pushed his arms into the sleeves.

"It's a bit big," Gannon said. "But you will grow into it soon enough."

As the weeks went by, Kieran and the old wizard became fast friends. Gannon taught the boy many spells and potions and tricks. Kieran could tell the stories whispered by the old oak trees and cross the river without getting wet—most of the time. He learned how to change mushrooms into drinking cups and flowers into doves—usually. As Kieran grew, he joined Gannon on his visits to the nearest village. They soothed the wounded with healing potions and astonished the children with their tricks. As the years went by, Kieran grew to be a great and noble wizard.

One day, as the old wizard rested against a tree in the meadow, Kieran knelt beside him. Old age had made Gannon frail. Kieran swept a spider's web from the tree and spun it into a thread with his fingers. He whispered a magic spell. "Wisps of spider's silky web, weave together for his bed."

Kieran shook out the spun thread until it was large enough to tuck around the old wizard. Gannon awoke and placed his winkled hand on Kieran's. "Many years ago, I gave you home and hearth and taught you the ways of magic. In return, you filled my life with wonder and joy. I have one last spell I'd like to teach you."

Gannon pulled a white feather from his robe and twirled it between his fingers before settling it in Kieran's hand. He picked up the braided tail of his beard. "A bird of flight, the color of light. To ease your loneliness..."

As the wizard closed his eyes to the world, the feather hovered above. Slowly it transformed into a pure white raven and perched on Kieran's outstretched arm. Eyes as blue as sapphires peered at Kieran, with the same wizened gaze that he had often received from his friend. Kieran gave a tearful chuckle, knowing the kind spirit of the old wizard was near.

Many years passed in the cottage of Kieran and his white raven, but one winter night when the moon was full and bright, the raven flew deep into the forest. He did not return the next dawn, or at noon, or at supper. Just as Kieran began to worry that he would never see his friend again, a knock sounded at the cottage door. When Kieran turned the latch, a small and ragged child stood in the shadow of the doorway.

"Please, sir," the little boy begged. "Could you spare a crust of bread?"

With gentle hands, Kieran pulled a white feather from the boy's curly locks. Twirling it between his fingers, he smiled. "I can do better than that."

Illustrations by Linda Ravenscroft
www.lindaravenscroft.com

About the illustrator

Patricia Ann Lewis-MacDougall started drawing as soon as she could hold a pencil and filled every blank spot in her mother's cook books by the age of three. She now tells stories with her love of drawing and has illustrated children's books and created storyboards for television animation for shows such as Little Bear and Franklin the Turtle. Pat Ann lives in Stoney Creek, Ontario. Visit her online at:

www.pat-ann.com

About the Author

Jennifer Carson lives in New Hampshire with her husband, four sons and many furred and feathered friends. She grew up on a steady diet of Muppet movies and Renaissance faires and would occasionally be caught reading under the blankets with a flashlight. Besides telling tales, Jennifer likes to create fantasy creatures and characters and publishes her own sewing patterns. Her artwork and patterns can be seen online at:

www.thedragoncharmer.com

Made in the USA
San Bernardino, CA
21 March 2014